The Dark Portal
By Kyle Belote

Copyright Page

Cover by: Ivan Zann
https://www.bookcoversart.com

Author's Socials:
Substack: www.outpostdire.com
X: @OutpostDire
Instagram: @Outpost_Dire

Works By The Author

Acknowledgements

To my beta readers, thank you for your patience, diligence, and feedback. I may craft the story, but you help mold it.

Dedication

I dedicate this book to those who've taken a leap of faith and picked up my works. Whether this is your first or only the next one in a series you've read, I thank you from the bottom of my heart. You're truly remarkable for it.

Foreword from the Author

This story takes place on an alien world with alien settings. Instead of introducing a whole new set of vocabulary and names for persons, places, or things, the colloquial terminology we are accustomed to has been transplanted for ease of reading.

Chapter 1: The Dome

Darrovan's slow inhale sounded like a rush of thunder in his ears. His muscles trembled with terror.

What's going to happen once the doors open?

The elevator's darkness, lit only by the soft red glow of the display panel, didn't help.

His scales shivered, and the razor sharp claws of his fingers extended in agitation. He had never been prone to claustrophobia, but the dim confines set him on edge.

Oh God, what did I do? Why are they doing this?

The lift put out the softest of hums, and he could scarcely feel the movement. Only the slight tug on his insides gave any indication of descent.

A soft chime notified him of the car's arrival, and the motion stilled.

His breath quickened.

The doors parted.

A flood of blinding light rushed forward.

Darrovan threw up a hand to shield his eyes, and his claws retracted. He blinked several times to adjust to the bright environment.

"Step out," a crisp male voice said.

The voice startled Darrovan, and he almost yelped. Again, his claws extended in fright, an evolutionary reaction. He fought for control and retracted them. It was bad manners to be seen with them elongated.

The sound of movement just beyond Darrovan's vision drew his attention.

Squinting, and with his heart hammering, Darrovan complied. His steps were slow, timid. Once free of the elevator, the doors hissed closed behind him. His head jerked at the sound.

No going back now; I'm trapped.

"Who are you?" that same voice snapped.

Darrovan spun back to the front, spying a helmeted individual to the left. His visor reflected a darker image of Darrovan's disheveled form. The doorman stood behind a podium, dressed in pale blue attire that resembled a hazard suit more than armor or dress code.

A finger of worry wiggled its way through Darrovan's gut.

I was right—they're going to kill me!

1

Darrovan tried to peer beyond the tinted visor, but couldn't discern any visual cues. Anonymity shrouded the figure. A gray badge hung over his left breast pocket, ensnaring Darrovan's skittish attention.

"Credentials," the other said, holding out a hand.

What's he talking about?

Darrovan stammered, "I—I don't have any."

His eyes flashed beyond the other person, soaking in what little details he could see. The chamber's appearance seemed as hospitable as the doorman.

The interior stretched out like a hangar, but a stale, crisp environment. The stark white room was almost square, a good twenty paces long and nearly as wide.

A large fountain with a broad base gurgled at the other end of the room. Potted plants and trees formed a ring around it. Darrovan wasn't sure, but the room appeared to extend beyond the other side of the decoration.

The doorman snapped his fingers.

Darrovan's head swiveled back to him.

"What do you mean you don't have credentials? Everyone is supposed to."

The faceless individual pulled on the gray emblem attached to his shirt and pressed a button on the desk. A hiss sounded from above. Darrovan's head snapped up. The ceiling parted, and two massive guns dropped down. They turned, zeroing on him. The multi-barrel weapons began to spin.

Oh, shit. Why are they doing this? Why am I here?

"All visitors are required to hand over credentials upon entrance to be verified—"

"Talcen!" another voice called out, this one from a female.

Her snapping stride preceded her arrival. She stepped into view, materializing behind one of the many pillars that lined the room.

Similar to the doorman's appearance, she wore the same pale blue color, but hers likened to that of a jumpsuit with a charcoal gray collar and cuffs on her sleeves. Her rosy complexion softened the white monotony around them. Like the first man, a small gray badge pinned to her torso was the only adornment on her clothing. Darrovan caught sight of the faint hologram of her appearance on the upper right corner as she stopped in front of him.

She flashed a smile towards Darrovan.

"Sorry about that."

She gazed at the first man, Talcen.

"We've been expecting Dr. Weiv's arrival. You can stand down."

"He doesn't have credentials," Talcen said with a monotone voice.

Man has a limited vocabulary. What the hell's up with him and credentials?

The woman stood straighter.

"Emergency orders override protocol. I've cleared him for entrance, so that's the last we should hear about it."

Talcen glanced from her to Darrovan. The dark visor centered on him for a moment longer than necessary for a cursory glance.

Darrovan's throat constricted.

Why's it so hard to swallow?

"As you wish," Talcen said at last.

He swiped his card and pushed an unseen button again. The weapons stopped spinning, swiveled, and rose into the ceiling. The plate hissed closed behind them, camouflaging their existence.

The woman turned her attention back to Darrovan and flashed an apologetic smile.

"Sometimes, I think the military puts out nothing but simpletons and drones. Sorry for his zealous nature. He takes security too seriously."

She dipped her head.

"I'm Sheedah, Head of Operations."

She extended a hand.

Not dead, not dead.

Darrovan reached out with a trembling hand.

"Pleasure to meet you," he said, his voice tremulous.

"Follow me."

Sheedah moved deeper into the room, towards the fountain.

He hurried after her. His legs wobbled with fatigue and the trepidation of knowing how close he came to dying. He swallowed, thanking whoever looked out for him for the stay of execution. He'd already thought once tonight that he was going to die. The run-in with Talcen made it two.

Darrovan peeked backward after a few paces and noted Talcen's visor turned in their direction, watching him go. It sent a shiver up his spine.

"Don't you worry about insulting the …"

"Sentry? Military member?"

She shook her head.

"No. Talcen isn't a people person—never mingles. People have been trying to get him to open up for years, but he never does. I don't ever recall seeing him without that helmet on."

She sighed.

"He's always on duty."

Darrovan shook his head at the news, trying to comprehend all the implications.

"I'm sorry, did you say years?"

Sheedah dipped her head in acknowledgment.

"Yes. Many of us have been down here a long time, but not as long as Lias."

"Lias?"

"Yes, the old man of the dome as we call him. He's the one who sent for you."

They reached the fountain, and a soft hum of music filtered through hidden speakers, hushed string instruments ranging in timbre and bass. Sheedah paused, her arm gesturing to the frothing water.

"Many of us come here when the walls feel like they're closing in."

She gestured up to the ceiling, and he followed the movement.

"The ceiling's one giant monitor that often carries the same color and mannerisms as the sky outside. Normally, it's on a bright, cheery setting, but you can catch the rain and snow at times."

She smiled.

"I don't mind seeing them, but I don't miss the weather."

Darrovan blinked a few times and shook his head again.

What does this have to do with anything?

He almost died, and she acted as if nothing was wrong. Who were these people? Where was he?

"I'm sorry," he said. "I'm not sure why I am here. I was dragged out of bed, rushed from my home in the middle of the night and thrown into—"

"Yes, I know," she spoke in a soothing voice.

She held up a hand to stop him, her dark eyes widening. Her magenta complexion darkened, a sign of embarrassment.

"All will be explained in due time."

Irritation flared through him, stifling the disquiet from earlier. "No, sorry, that's not good enough. I want to know—"

"We can't discuss it here," Sheedah said, her eyes flitting over to Talcen, who still watched them. "Not everyone has clearance for such things."

She tapped the gray card on her chest.

"We've all got key cards to signify who's authorized. You've got to learn the colors."

She jerked her head in a direction behind her and to the left.

"Come on, there's a lot to learn and discuss."

Darrovan suppressed a sigh.

He almost refused to go any further until he got answers, but Sheedah was moving away, and he didn't want to be left with Talcen.

Darrovan glanced back at the military member.

Just my luck, he'd be trigger happy, too.

He followed his guide.

Today couldn't be any more bizarre. When he went to sleep, he hadn't expected a home invasion.

At first, he thought he was being kidnapped, but who would kidnap a professor of metaphysics and alien theory? His second inclination had been the authorities had come to seize him for heresy. He wouldn't put it past the fascist government to silence him for dissent. But the captors turned out to be military, and he wasn't entirely sure that was any better.

In the panic of the moment, when they encircled him in his bedroom with weapons drawn, they stuffed an envelope in his coat pocket, and threw a sack over his head. On the ride over, they gave strict instructions to not open it before he arrived. He should've known then they weren't going to kill him, but he didn't have any expectations of how executions played out.

"The badges," Sheedah said, breaking into his thoughts as they walked, "represent the level of clearance. The white areas of the dome are open to everyone of any clearance. All hallways are white, but the rooms attached may not be, so no wandering. The green badges access only the green spaces, and the same for the other colors."

"Other colors?"

"Yes, in order of clearance level, they are green, yellow, red, and blue. Gray's for administrators and has blue clearance. Black for the overseer and those of the highest clearance. Conversely, a higher color has the clearance to be privy of everything below."

Darrovan remembered her gray insignia and her title.

"So, who's got a black badge?"

"Lias, the old man of the dome, and a handful of others."

"But not you? Aren't you the Head of Operations?"

She shot a wistful, sidelong smile at him.

"Yes, I am, and no, not yet."

"Yet?"

The doors parted as they approached, and they entered the hallway beyond. The first doorframe on the left glowed green. Darrovan cast a glance down the hall and noted the others were green as well. Several rows of tubes ran the length of the passageway and over the doorframes, the bottom one glowed green, too.

"In here."

She pointed to the door.

"We'll get you access."

Darrovan stepped inside and expected another sentry like Talcen, but the room remained devoid of any lifeforms. White, hard plastic chairs lined the wall near the door. The room was almost free of adornment save for a potted plant in the far corner, and a painting of a ship on high seas. A receptacle station sat in the middle, its display coming to life as it detected movement within the room.

"Please insert your badge," it said as he neared it.

"I don't have one."

"Please place your hand on the screen. We will take a DNA scan."

DNA? Oh God, they're going to put me in a system, track all my movements.

Darrovan cast a glance at Sheedah, who nodded encouragement. With a sigh and grudging reluctance, he pressed a hand to the display.

"Welcome, Professor Darrovan Wiev."

His brow twitched.

"How did—?"

"Please open the envelope in your possession at this time," the terminal said.

The annoyance Darrovan pushed down earlier rose again. There were too many unanswered questions. Where was he? Why was he here? How did they have his DNA in their databanks already? How did the terminal know he had an envelope?

He reached inside the coat's pocket and pulled out the crumpled paper. It was soft, like the insides were coated with bubble wrap. Angry red slash marks covered the edge of the sleeve. In bold print, a warning sprawled across the surface:

[Attn: Dorrovan Wiev. For Official Use Only. Do Not Tamper.]

He held the wrapping to the light, finding the edge of the paper inside, if there was any—he didn't see one—and tore the envelope's end. Reversing the packet, the contents dumped into his awaiting hand.

A small black card encased in hardened transparisteel rested in his palm. Sheedah inhaled. He looked up, finding her eyes wide.

"What?"

"I expected a red, maybe blue, but never black."

That finger of worry grew into a shard of anxiety and stabbed him in the gut. What was he doing here? Why all the cloak and dagger?

"Please place your badge on the screen," the terminal prompted.

He slapped the identification on the display, and the monitor flashed a few times.

"Accepted. Authorization level: Black. Access granted to all areas of the facility. If your badge is lost or stolen, please report it to the nearest wall-comm unit. Your misplaced card will be locked out, and a new one will be made for you. Be advised that all information discussed must be done in the appropriate designated areas. Enjoy your stay."

The screen went dark, and Darrovan picked up the token with a groan.

"What? Is this place a resort or something? Seems more like a hospital or a prison."

"In some ways it's a resort," Sheedah said, her voice soft with a touch of envy. "There's an entertainment level for off-time. Having amenities lets people unwind."

"Alright," he said, tapping the badge in his hand. He rolled his eyes. "I have access. So, tell me what's going on."

She shook her head.

"Not yet. We're in a green room."

She beckoned for him to follow and turned for the door. He clenched his fist, wadded up what was left of the envelope, and stuffed it into the right side pocket.

In the hallway, Sheedah continued.

"You must wear your identification at all times. For now, just carry it in your hands. When we come up to a door, hold it up for the cameras to read. It won't be an issue much longer. We'll give you some new clothes, and you can attach it to the attire."

He stopped in the middle of the hallway.

"Wait, hold on," he said.

She turned and gave a quizzical look.

"Change of clothes? Exactly how long do you expect me to stay here?"

The speakers overhead crackled to life with a faint hum.

"As long as necessary, Professor Wiev."

Darrovan scanned up at the sound of the smooth, male voice, searching for the origin. He didn't find the speakers, but he did find a small, almost unnoticeable alcove where the ceiling met the wall.

That's just great. I'm being stalked by Big Brother.

"Who are you?" he asked.

"That's Lias, the Chief Executive," Sheedah answered. She peered down the hall. "It's just a little further to the lift, and then we can answer all your questions."

Another elevator. The last one didn't inspire confidence, and when he exited, Talcen held him at gunpoint. What awaited on the other side of the next one?

"What if I say no?" Darrovan countered, a small sliver of defiance rising within him.

"That would be unwise," Lias said over the speaker, "and I'll just have Talcen deliver you to me."

Great. Talcen's not only the doorman but an enforcer.

Sheedah took a step closer and dropped her voice.

"Please, it's only a little further."

"How do I know I'm not marching to my death or detainment?"

Lias chuckled. "We wouldn't've gone through all this trouble to kill you, Professor Wiev."

"Imprisonment then?"

Humor came from the speakers. "Killing you would be cheaper. No, no, we need your mind intact, and your cooperation."

Further down the hall, the doors to the lift parted. A soft golden glow shined across the reflective, polished floor.

"Please?" Sheedah coaxed.

With a sigh, Darrovan followed her to the lift. She entered, and he stepped in behind her. Darrovan glanced at the buttons inside. Thirteen floors were listed, and the glow around the first floor lit up. The doors closed, and they ascended.

A plethora of scenarios flooded through him. While Lias assured they didn't mean him harm, how could he trust the voice? He had to admit, it was a somewhat convoluted way to kill him. The personnel who invaded his home could've dispatched with him, shot him while he slept, staged it as a robbery gone wrong.

The list was endless.

But what worried him the most was the talk about needing his mind intact. What did that even mean? If anything, it sounded like an experiment from a crazed scientist. The image of a laser cutting into his skull to extract his brain didn't help the rising anxiety.

When the doors parted again, a dark room lay beyond.

Yeah, nothing creepy about that.

There was ample light, but the black floors and walls gave the impression of little illumination. Unlike all the other rooms he'd seen thus far, this one spanned out in a circular fashion.

Numerous glass panes broke up and relieved the darkness. Light flooded in from beyond. Tubes of different hues pulsed around the room, the same colors as the badges.

"Welcome to the observatory," Lias called from somewhere within.

Darrovan stepped out of the elevator and felt Sheedah stepping with him. He gave a quick glance at her, noting she wasn't armed.

Well, that's something.

Inside, the black floor gleamed with a polished luster. Most of the desks mirrored the floor but with charcoal gray edges. The running lights near the floor and high above glowed, washing the room in a prism-like ambiance.

Darrovan stepped further into the room, turning, taking in the view.

Monitors of all sizes, with displays he could only guess the meaning of, surrounded the entire room. Workstations, with chairs pushed under the desks, stood aligned in military precision. Still, despite the orderly appearance, the place screamed cluttered.

He stepped closer to a monitor, this one displaying a global map in two-dimension. Lines crisscrossed the surface in different colors. Red, blue, white, yellow, green, all the colors of the badges, and more. He even spied a purple line where red and blue converged.

"They're trunk lines for optic cables," Sheedah advised from behind him.

A noise drew his attention, and he turned to the center of the room. A short, balding man with a cane hobbled into view. Darrovan's eyes drew to the long, wispy beard he sported. Its length attested to the dedication Lias had. His ethnicity wasn't known for robust facial hair.

His scales gleamed a touch too oily to be healthy, and their once-brilliant red sheen had paled to a faded pink. Indeed, Sheedah hadn't been lying when she proclaimed Lias as the old man of the dome.

When Lias came to a stop in front of Darrovan, he planted the cane in front of him and extended a greeting.

"I trust you have many more questions now."

The professor didn't sense any hostility from the man, and his scent implied as much. If anything, he impressed a genial and eager attitude.

Darrovan nodded, his gaze sweeping in a slow arch across the chamber.

"What is this place?"

"A restricted and covert department," Lias began. "It was first a top-secret military base long ago in the Geban Wars. They relinquished the facility, and it was bought up by private companies, or so the story goes. A private business did manage to buy up the underground facilities before the military swooped in and bought up everything topside. They used shell companies, of course. They let the remains of the base fall into disuse. Eventually, time and covert destruction did the rest."

"Geban Wars?" Darrovan echoed. "That was what? Some three-hundred years ago?"

"Three-hundred and seven to be exact," Lias corrected, his finger lifting off the cane for emphasis.

"So, what happened to the private company?"

"Hmm? Oh, well, they were bought out by another shell company. So, the military has had this place ever since they 'relinquished' control."

Darrovan shook his head, flabbergasted. "But why?"

"Appearances had to be kept," Sheedah slipped into the conversation. "After the Geban Wars and what they had to do to ensure resounding victory, well, public opinion soured against the military. The government offered up this base as a scapegoat."

"And now, we operate in secret," Lias finished.

He waved a hand.

"As you can see, the interior isn't as old as the topside. It's been refurbished with the latest technology. We are a state-of-the-art complex."

Darrovan let out a long sigh and shook his head.

"Alright, so what does that have to do with me, and why am I here?"

His lips thinned.

"You could've picked up the phone and invited me instead of scaring me to death."

"No, we couldn't," Sheedah commented. "The government's tapping your phone."

Anger and fear welled up within him. The government was keeping tabs on him? Why? Surely his profession wasn't deemed as dangerous or inciting to dissenters.

Paranoia flooded him, and felt cold and clammy.

How long had they been listening? What had he said on the line that could be construed as dissidence? What caused them to start tapping his phone?

Lias cocked his head.

"Do you remember reading about that catastrophe during the early years of space exploration? Something about how they captured a small meteor and brought it back for testing?"

Darrovan nodded, still too numb to speak.

Shit, maybe they will kill me after all.

"That was here."

He blinked, the words registering.

"Here?"

Lias nodded.

"Oh yes, quite calamitous. Killed the entire research team in the explosion."

"This place looks and sounds like the embodiment of bad luck."

"It never happened," Sheedah explained.

Darrovan's eyes widened, then narrowed as he glanced between them.

"What do you mean? The explosion? The meteor? What?"

"Oh, no," Lias said, "that happened. The explosion really did kill all those scientists, but there was never a meteor."

A short silence filled the air between them, and curiosity prickled Darrovan's chest.

"Alright, what was it?"

"We don't know," Lias admitted.

Darrovan crossed his arms.

"Really? Or you just can't say?"

Lias shrugged.

"Both, perhaps."

The short, old man eyed Sheedah for a moment.

"Would you excuse us, darling?"

Sheedah dipped her head.

"Of course. I'll prepare the professor's room. Send him down once you've finished."

"That would be wonderful, thank you," Lias said.

Darrovan watched her go.

Once Sheedah entered the elevator and left, Lias continued. "She can't be privy to this conversation. It requires level black clearance after all, but something did happen here. How and why has yet to be determined. Ever since that fateful day, the miasma has remained."

Darrovan blinked.

"I'm sorry, what? A miasma?"

"That's what most of the other scientists call it."

Lias cleared his throat.

"Some are far more superstitious and think it's a nexus of spirits come back to haunt the living. Others theorize it's the remains of some government experiment gone wrong."

Lias hefted the cane and rolled it in his fingers, eyeing the handle that resembled their world.

"I call it The Dark Portal."

Chapter 2: The Infirmary

"The Dark Portal?" Darrovan echoed.

What the hell's a dark portal?

Lias announced it like something grandiose and ominous, but the delivery fell flat. Darrovan couldn't deny his intrigue, though. It sounded both sinister and a code word for a military experiment.

Maybe some new electromagnetic attack to knock out all the power?

Lias shrugged.

"It's a dramatic flair, sure, but that's what it reminds me of."

Darrovan swallowed, and he could feel his pulse shooting through his neck.

Of all the things he expected this evening, this wasn't it—to be privy to military operations. He had expected death or imprisonment. He could imagine rotting in a cell somewhere, forgotten.

The government was run by fanatics, and he wouldn't put it past them to round up people they saw as threats to their rule. To be fair, they had mellowed over the last few decades, more to the military's threat than anything. But there was still a quiver of fear running rampant through the population.

People still disappeared.

If someone spoke too loudly of their dissent or criticized too harshly, they were eradicated. Of course, the government denied such knowledge, but the people knew the truth.

Why do politicians think the masses are dumb and naive?

The governing body moved swiftly to stifle opinions that didn't match their own. Too much free-thinking would be the death of their iron grip. Only the military stood immune, keeping those maniacal, power-hungry individuals in check. From what little Darrovan knew, the military dictated through their morals and code of honor, a stark contrast to the statesmen.

More than once, when a presiding legislator grew too incisive, the military responded with their own silencing techniques. If caught between the ruling body and the military, Darrovan chose the latter.

I guess I should consider myself lucky to be here. As bad as it is, it could be worse.

Darrovan cleared his throat.

"Who made this … portal, the military?"

Lias sighed and pointed to a chair.

"Do you mind if I sit? My leg's acting up."

"No, please. By all means."

"Thank you."

Lias hobbled over to the chair. Darrovan realized the chief executive didn't need to ask permission, but the small social request spoke volumes about the man's propriety.

Darrovan filed the information away for later. The old man of the dome was in charge yet humble enough to ask.

I should treat him with the same kindness he showed me.

When he sat, Lias let out a weary groan.

"Ah, that's better."

He stroked his beard with fingers combing through the fibrous hairs.

"No one really knows who made the portal. All the mad scientists with their lab coats have theories. I have my own."

Darrovan fidgeted.

He doesn't know who made the portal? I thought the military did.

"What's your theory?"

"Someone or something else made the Dark Portal."

The statement hung between them, and the implications came rushing. He took a deep breath.

"Something?"

Lias nodded.

"Something not of this world or the sothor race."

Darrovan blanched. His heart fluttered.

"You think it's something otherworldly, something alien?"

Lias stamped the cane on the floor.

"Yes, hence why we called on you, Professor."

The younger man shifted weight between his feet. The fine scales on his back stiffened.

"Where does this Dark Portal go?"

"I don't know," Lias admitted. "It may not go anywhere. None of the other scientists want to get close to it anymore, not after—"

Oh, God, what happened?

"After?"

The old man grimaced.

"My nephew, Calistor. The portal reacted when he got too close. It scrambled his brain, and now he can only speak gibberish when he isn't completely catatonic."

Darrovan's throat tightened. If this thing was something alien, who knew what it was doing to the man's nephew.

He's lucky to be alive at all.

A rush of realization washed over him. He was a professor of alien theory, and Lias thought this Dark Portal was extraterrestrial in origin, which meant the old man wanted him to study it.

His palms turned sweaty.

That means getting close to it.

A stab of fear lanced his chest.

What if the same thing happens to me?

He scrambled for something to say, anything to get his mind off what he might have to do.

"Have you told his family?"

Lias shook his head.

"My daughter and I are the only family he has left."

"Your daughter?"

Lias gave a harrumph.

"It's no wonder why you let your mind meander through the mystics of metaphysics and alien theory. You have no scent for what's right before your eyes."

The snub about his sense of smell rankled him, but only because it was close to the truth. As a species evolved from aquatic origins, smell played a significant role in evolution and breeding.

"Sheedah?" Darrovan asked, surprised.

Lias nodded.

"Yes."

Damn, how did I miss that?

"I should've known."

"Yes, you should have. It's hard to suppress the geban gene."

Darrovan felt the full weight of Lias's gaze, and a disquiet lanced the younger man.

"Are you going to have a problem working for me?" the old man asked.

Shit, not this same old stuff again.

Darrovan shook his head.

"Why would I?"

"Well, the geban and karfrie don't exactly have the best of history, and the wars are evidence of that."

Darrovan swallowed and fought back resignation.

"That was a long time ago—before you or I were ever born."

The old man smiled.

"Probably before five generations back were born."

Darrovan shrugged.

"I can't hold you accountable for the actions of your ancestors; no geban can hold the karfrie accountable for ancient atrocities. It's in the past, where it should be."

"Astute, and well said—especially coming from a man of your colorful credentials."

Darrovan rolled his eyes, expecting another ribbing about his chosen career.

Lias scratched his jaw.

"What made you choose metaphysics and alien theory, Professor?"

Darrovan chuckled at the ludicrous change in the line of questioning, but the tightness in his chest eased.

"Besides finding psychology boring? It was the last thing to still be explored, the vast unknown. We've mapped our ocean floors, established underwater settlements and colonies on our moons and nearby planets. There's nothing left to discover. What better way than hope for the best by searching for the unproven?"

"Well," Lias said, picking up the cane again and inspecting the globe handle, "perhaps now we have. Or rather, will."

His body prickled with sweat as they returned to the subject he dreaded.

"The Dark Portal?"

Lias nodded.

"The Dark Portal."

"Tell me about it."

"It isn't static like a doorway or anything. In fact, it's a dark, boiling cloud. It expands and contracts like an erratic set of lungs. We can't calculate the density, and we can't be sure, but some of us think a presence emanates from it."

"Presence?"

His brow rose as sharply as his heart rate.

Lias nodded, and his lips twisted.

"Others describe it as a guarded curiosity. I think it's more malevolent in design."

The implications boggled Darrovan's mind. Something alien or alien-made had an aura about it? He stammered the only thing he could think.

"That's assuming it's intelligent."

"Oh, it is. We've tested it."

"How?"

Lias shrugged.

"A simple multiple choice. We placed placards in front of it with colors. Said their names out loud and pointed, then called the colors at random. Each time, a tentacle pointed out the ones we called. Not the most sophisticated, but it worked given a language barrier."

Darrovan rubbed his fingers idly over the black badge. He felt sick, and his knees grew weak again.

"So, it's learning."

Lias cocked his head.

"Do you want to see it, Professor?"

The thought of him ending up catatonic gave rise to his initial impulse.

Hell no!

But he nodded instead.

"Yes, but I want to see your nephew first. What's his name?"

"Calistor. He's in the infirmary. What do you expect to learn from him?"

Darrovan gave a timid shake of the head.

"I haven't the slightest, to be honest, but it's a place to start, and it'll help me work up the nerve to visit the Dark Portal."

A lopsided grin spread across Lias's face.

"Very well."

The old man stood and extended a hand.

"Welcome aboard, Professor. We can talk more details later if you wish. I doubt we've scratched the surface of your questions, so my door's always open."

He pointed with the cane.

"Head back to the elevator and to the quarters level. It's two levels down on floor three. Change into the attire we provide and take the lift to the infirmary on level four."

Darrovan nodded and turned to leave.

Lias called out, "Oh, and Professor? Not a word about the details of your assignment to anyone not wearing a black badge. Not even my daughter."

He paused, finding it odd that Sheedah wasn't privy to potentially the most significant discovery of their species.

"She doesn't know?"

Lias shrugged.

"She's a smart woman and probably put snippets of information together, but not the full extent."

Darrovan took this information in stride, gave a single nod, and departed the observatory.

The lift deposited him on the quarter's floor. He exited and glanced left and right, noted the green lights running the length of the walls, and spied Sheedah standing in a doorway to the left. This level, like the main level, ran with white walls.

He ambled over to her.

When he came close, she stepped to the side.

"This is your room. You'll find all the amenities inside. Your clothes are in the closet."

Darrovan glanced within.

The room was small, maybe fifteen feet by twelve. It mirrored the hallway's color, the same monotonous hue. A doorway led off to the left and another to the right, the latter dumping into a closet. A bed scarcely larger than a cot sat against the far wall. Shelves encompassed the mattress, built under and around the sides of the bunk.

He stepped through the threshold and peered to the left, finding a small bathroom inside. He glanced back at Sheedah.

"It's not much," she said, the apology lacing her voice. "But the furniture's built on gliders, and you can collapse your bed, move your shelves, and pull out a desk if you need."

He nodded, his gaze sweeping the room. On the wall opposite the bed, a pull-down table sat upright. Upon closer inspection, he noted the same hard, white plastic from the chairs on the main floor. That, too, folded down like the table.

A question formed, and he kicked himself for not asking Lias.

Instead, he eyed Sheedah and asked, "How long do you expect me to stay here?"

She shrugged.

"As long as necessary."

"What about people's families? Their lives?"

Her lips twisted in a half-hearted apology.

"People *can* bring their families. Exceptions can be made for the most brilliant minds, of course. We try to provide many amenities. This place is set up to be a fully functioning community."

She eyed him.

"I don't know whether to breathe a sigh of relief that you're single, or to say I'm sorry about the lack of family."

His brow frowned, but he sidestepped her inquiry into his life.

"You mean they bring children here? To live in this walled environment?"

Her head bobbed an affirmation.

"Yes, of course, if need be. Not everyone has grown young ones. The children can play with others and develop crucial social skills."

He shook his head in disbelief, coming to the question he wanted answered most but feared the revelation.

"Has anyone ever left?"

Her face blanked.

"I can't answer that."

"'Cause you don't know, or don't want to give me the wrong impression?"

"Because only Lias deals with the dismissals."

"You mean your father?"

Her eyes widened in shock, and she rushed inside the apartment. She glanced back through the open doorway, searching for anyone who might be walking by.

"He told you?"

Darrovan nodded.

She took a deep breath.

"Well, Professor, I trust you'll keep that information to yourself. No one else knows, and no one has been allowed family members to work with them."

He arched a brow, sarcasm tainting his tone.

"Preferential treatment? Nepotism? Color me shocked. How did you sneak this tidbit past the others?"

Sheedah, still acting skittish, took a deep breath.

"I use my mother's name."

She rubbed her forehead.

"Please change. Once you're finished, I'll take you wherever you want to go."

She stepped out, and the door slid shut.

Darrovan did a slow turn in the room. Just as stark as the rest of the place, it left much to be desired. He hoped he didn't have to stay long, but he wondered if others were allowed to customize their rooms.

A bit of color and decor would make it homier.

Tired and weary, he changed in haste and stepped out of the room a few minutes later. Sheedah leaned closer once he exited and helped pin the black card to his shirt.

"It's tricky," she said.

It attached to a clasp anchored on a small round housing. Once connected, she pulled on the badge, showing him it extended out. She let go and the chord wound back up into the unit, and the identification dangled on his chest.

"Where to?" she asked.

"The infirmary."

Her brow rose, but she didn't say anything else.

A few moments later, they exited the lift on the infirmary level, which dumped out into a medical foyer. Some doctors milled about, glancing up at their arrival.

Darrovan didn't grasp much about the medical field, but the first room in front of the elevator resembled a minor treatment facility. The room was circular, and glass panels lined the room from floor to ceiling. A patient bed sat in the middle. Along the back wall was a countertop and cupboards for various medicines and surgical equipment.

Sheedah stepped to the right and guided him to Calistor's room beyond the foyer.

Yellow tubes of light accentuated the bright white walls and ran the length. He noted other containers, too, no doubt to change the color based on their needs.

They stepped to the doorway of Calistor's room. The crew within glanced up at their arrival. Darrovan eyed them, noting their badges. Some were blue, but most were red.

His eyes tracked deeper into the room, seeing a young man lying on a bed. Calistor didn't move. Wires riddled his body. A monitor beeped in a steady cadence.

"He's been catatonic," Sheedah said quietly.

Darrovan didn't respond, eyes still lingering on Calistor. He couldn't make out his features, but he was surprised the patient didn't possess the geban appearance like Lias and Sheedah. If anything, he looked more amdulan in ethnicity for his prominent, yellow sheen and glistening scales.

The professor half hoped the young man would be conscious and rambling. He might have learned something. Questions flooded his mind. What had the portal done to him? What did it feel like?

Lias's words floated through Darrovan's mind.

"Professor? Not a word about the details of your assignment to anyone not wearing a black badge. Not even my daughter."

"Everybody out," Darrovan said.

One female doctor with a blue badge stiffened, her face bristling, but she nodded encouragement to the others, and they departed without argument.

The doctor stopped in front of him. This close, he noticed her attractiveness, and he hated himself for starting off on the wrong foot. Her eyes darted to his black badge. As she did, he did a quick cursory glance of her, the sparkle of her cheek scales, the vibrancy of her vertical pupil eyes, and her generous womanly features on a lean frame.

"I trust you've got a good excuse for interrupting our work?"

Sheedah held out a hand for introductions.

"Dr. Brelo, this is Professor Darrovan Wiev. Darrovan, Dr. Brelo."

The professor extended his hand, and the doctor hesitated, then shook it.

"Indeed, I do," he assured. "I won't be long, I promise."

Mollified, Brelo left. He watched her leave, reaffirming how beautiful he found her. He shook his head. She probably hated him now, or at the very least, found him annoying.

Darrovan turned to Sheedah.

"That includes you."

Indignation flashed across her face, but he cut her off by tapping the card on his chest.

"It's like you said, can't talk to people who aren't the same clearance level, right?"

Her lips thinned, and she gave a stiff nod. She, too, left.

Darrovan waded deeper into the room, coming up beside the young man covered in a thin white sheet. The scene reminded him of those holodramas where the law enforcement and medical personnel performed autopsies. He half expected to see an incision along his thorax but was relieved not to find one.

As he neared, Darrovan placed his hands on the side of the bed. From all appearances, the young man lay asleep. What answers did he expect to find from a slumbering patient?

God, what did it do to you?

A disconcerting thought came to him. What if the same thing happened to him?

His legs trembled.

Would the crew have experience in what to do? He hoped they wouldn't cut off life support, but if he was in pain, he'd want an end to it.

Would they even realize if I was in pain?

For a brief moment, an impulse arced within. The urge to pull the plug and let Calistor fade washed over him. His hand twitched in the direction of the machine.

What the hell am I doing?

He pulled his hand back.

21

What had come over him? What drove him to even consider it? He couldn't do that to Calistor. If he did, Lias would surely order his execution. But was it not a kindness to do what the family could not?

He shook his head, staring at a possible future version of himself. A knot formed in his stomach. What was the Dark Portal, and how did it generate this kind of power? What if the same thing happened to him and scrambled his brain? Would he forget everything he knew? How did this happen?

Darrovan noted Calistor's face. He didn't appear to be a relative to Lias and Sheedah. Perhaps that was a good thing. If too many looked like the old man of the dome, they might suspect their blatant nepotism. But it did beg the question as to why Lias had chosen family members other than the obvious.

I wonder if he regrets that now. Maybe that's why he called me?

He shook the dark thought away.

His gaze flickered to Calistor's closed eyes. His lids fluttered, the eyeballs moving beneath. Did the young man dream? If so, what haunted him? What escape did he seek?

Darrovan knew little of the medical field, but at least the brain was still active.

"Calistor?" Darrovan spoke softly.

If the young man woke, he didn't want to startle him overmuch.

"Calistor?" he tried again, a touch louder.

When the patient didn't respond to further prodding, Darrovan accepted temporary defeat. He could come back. Lias had said Calistor did ramble. Maybe Darrovan would catch him awake one of these days.

There was nothing left to learn, at least not now. Without wasting any more time, Darrovan turned and left the infirmary.

Chapter 3: The Vault

When he exited the infirmary, the doctors glanced up. His eyes tracked to Brelo—the one he found attractive. His facial scales quivered with infatuation. She held his gaze, but the hardness of her earlier irritation couldn't be found.

"May we resume our duties?" she asked, overlooking the slight tell.

He was grateful she didn't make a scene. Morose, he nodded, and the medical team filed into Calistor's room. His eyes flickered to Brelo as she passed, and he caught a small smile on her lips.

Sheedah hadn't budged; she leaned against the wall with a mix of mild curiosity and despondence.

"Find what you are looking for?" she queried.

"No. Not yet."

"Yet? There is no yet. He's gone, Professor."

He shook his head.

"No, he's not."

"But the medical team—"

"He may be absent for the time being," Darrovan interrupted, tapping his temple, "but he's still in there."

He paused, regarding her.

"That's rather callous of you, all things considered."

He lifted a brow, expectant.

She ignored the comment.

"What makes you so sure?"

"He's dreaming."

Sheedah took this answer in silence. Her head wobbled as she considered what he said.

"Where to now?"

"The portal."

"The portal?" Sheedah asked, her voice rising in confusion.

Darrovan winced.

Damn, she doesn't know.

He stammered, "Where the scientists are—the black area. Take me there."

Sheedah nodded.

"You want the vault."

She didn't say anything else on the subject and led him to the lift. Once inside, she pressed the last button.

"Identification, please," the elevator said.

Sheedah motioned to him. He blinked a few times before realizing what she wanted. He stepped close and tugged on his identification card. The thin metal wire extended as he held the badge to the plate.

The lift chimed.

"Thank you, Professor."

The doors closed, and they descended.

He took a deep breath and prepared himself for the unexpected. Several scenarios ran rampant through his mind, most ending horribly. Perhaps the paranoia bred into him by living under a totalitarian government, or being the guest of a brutal covert military played a role.

A part of him still clung to the possibility of an elaborate hoax or ruse. In the back of his mind, imprisonment or execution percolated. While he firmly believed in his chosen career, and in the probability of extraterrestrials, to face one was something he never considered a genuine prospect.

By the time the doors parted, his insides writhed like worms.

A small chamber greeted him. Not five paces away stood a massive metal door. The imposing barrier appeared heavy and thick, a door able to stop gunfire. Darrovan stepped out but eyed Sheedah when she didn't move.

"This is as far as I go."

His brow frowned.

"What's to keep you from exiting the elevator?"

She gave him a lopsided grin, one that made him feel stupid for asking, but she did well to keep the condescension out of her voice.

"If I step out, the elevator will mark my exit."

She fingered her badge.

"The outer door to the room will lock, and not even your identification will make it unlock, not until I get back in the elevator."

The professor nodded at the sensible security measure. Still, she'd been with him all this time, and he'd grown content with her presence. Facing the extraterrestrial alone didn't help soothe his growing anxiousness.

Sheedah cleared her throat.

"I have duties to attend. I'm sure you can find your way from here."

Darrovan nodded, and Sheedah pressed a button on the panel. The elevator doors closed, and the soft whirl of the lift ascending filled the silence.

Loneliness closed around him, something frigid and uncomfortable. A claw of dread wrapped around his heart as the hum faded into nothing. In the absence of sound, a soft ring filled his ears, and he could again hear his breathing.

Not for the first time, the thought of being expendable shot through his soul. Casualties were expected in war, but not science experiments. When encountering a new species, precautions were expected, both for the observer and the animal. Now, he felt like a victim of a calamitous operation.

He turned back to the gunmetal door.

The soft glow of the card reader to the right filled his vision.

His throat constricted.

Whatever lay beyond had Lias worried. He'd called it alien. Whatever it was, it learned and put Calistor in the infirmary.

He took a deep breath through his nose and crossed the distance to the panel. He slapped the badge against the device.

"Welcome, Professor."

The locks clanked, and the door hissed opened. It yawned ponderously, and Darrovan knew his first assessment of the door's durability missed the mark. The thick hatch was almost as long as his arm.

That thing could survive a demolition blast or a missile!

Then, a dark thought filled him with dread.

Maybe it's not meant to keep people out, but trap something in?

As he stepped through, he noted the walls.

No, this was a bomb shelter built to withstand bombardment.

With a pang of anxiety, he realized his appraisal was correct, the perfect place to keep this otherworldly creature inside, along with anyone else who had been compromised.

What if I'm the one who gets exposed and infected?

His thoughts flickered back to Calistor and questioned the wisdom of keeping a contaminated worker in the infirmary with the doctors.

Brelo filled his mind.

It was a security risk. If the Dark Portal had contaminated Calistor, then anyone who came in contact with him might be susceptible, Darrovan included. The notion did not sit well with him.

That's something to bring up to Lias. He's not going to like that.

Once he passed through the portal, the door began to close before opening all the way.

Must be a sensor somewhere.

The hatch hissed back into place. Another door, still metal but not as bulky, swung open at a lumbering rate. The black color was not lost on him, a not-too-subtle reminder of entering a secured area.

Does the black paint hide the scorch marks from that explosion Lias talked about?

He hid a cringe and stepped through, expecting the room to be black and dark, but the floors and walls were bathed in stark white. A black band of paint at the top and bottom of the walls gave the only relief.

Heads turned in his direction, scientists perking up from their stations. Confusion and alarm stole across their features.

One tall, lean male hurried over. A touch of anger covered his features, and Darrovan expected a rebuke, but the scientist noted the black badge and seemed mollified.

"Welcome," he said in a soft, high tone.

He sounded like an adolescent still wading through puberty.

"I'm Guinnian, the lead researcher."

"Darrovan Weiv," the professor said, extending his hand.

Guinnian regarded the outstretched hand for a moment as if unsure what to do. After the moment of awkwardness passed, Guinnian returned the gesture.

"Ah, the professor of alien conspiracies? We told Lias we needed more help, not a conspiracy theorist."

What did he just say?

Guinnian paused, steepling long fingers in front of him. His pale green sheen marked him as a blagren, as did the two protrusions on the top of his head, small hardened bone resembling tall knots rather than horns.

He fidgeted.

"Sorry, that was rather rude of me."

He spread his arms.

"I'm ill-fitted for socializing. They usually just keep me locked away so I don't scare off the sponsors."

Darrovan frowned, his brow drawing down.

"You mean, you actually let people come here?"

"Of course not!" he snapped, taken aback by what he perceived as Darrovan's blatant stupidity.

The lead researcher waved a hand in a shooing motion.

"At the old research facility. As luck has it, we don't have to worry about that here."

"Hmm."

"Conspiracies isn't the right word."

"Sorry?"

"Your profession is alien theory, correct?"

"Yes."

Guinnian turned and waved behind him.

"I don't know how much help you'll be."

Niether do I.

He stopped in mid-motion.

"Sorry, again, rude. The subtleties of social interactions are rather lost on me."

"Hmm."

"It's a condition."

"What kind?"

"The mental one."

Guinnian continued waving behind him.

"We're the brightest minds across the nation in our diverging fields, and even we are baffled by the miasma."

"What fields?"

Guinnian snapped his head back around.

"What?"

"Your fields of study, what are they?"

Guinnian paused, steepling fingers under his chin to keep himself from fidgeting.

"Strange."

"What is?"

"You express a desire to learn about that which you have no knowledge. How does this help you?"

"I was being polite, making conversation, familiarizing myself with the others and their areas of expertise."

Guinnian's black eyes widened, and his facial scales vibrated.

"Ah, I see! Rude again. I apologize."

He tapped the ends of his fingers, twitching.

"Yes, well, we have a geneticist, a chemist, a microbiologist, an ethologist—"

"Hang on, why would you need someone who studied animal behavior?"

Guinnian paused, eyes darting back and forth, unsure of how to conduct himself after being interrupted. The scales on his neck vibrated with agitation.

"In case it's alive."

Darrovan frowned but nodded and chose not to interrupt again.

"Is that all of them?"

"No, there are more to varying degrees, but those are the more prominent ones."

"And you?"

"What?"

"What's your field of study?"

"Ah, a physicist," Guinnian answered in a tone that left Darrovan with the impression he should've known that tidbit already.

The professor nodded, more out of polite uncertainty than anything.

"Want to introduce me to the others?"

"Whatever for?"

"Well ..." Darrovan paused, baffled. "You're the lead researcher."

"Yes, I am."

Darrovan suppressed a sigh. His claws twitched, partially extended before sliding back into his fingertips. He had no doubt Guinnian was a brilliant individual, but the lack of social skills whittled his composure.

Further interactions with this windbag will be unfruitful.

Darrovan smiled a tight grin that didn't reach his eyes. The discomfort of their dialogue made him want to escape.

"I'll just go and introduce myself to them, shall I?"

"But, you'll interrupt their work."

"I'm sure they won't mind a few moments to get to know the stranger who just walked into the room."

"Ah," Guinnian said, steepling fingers under his chin again. "Yes, manners. That seems right."

Guinnian departed, his tall, lean form striding with a slight hunch. He seemed to stoop from the weight of his brain.

Darrovan shook his head.

All that knowledge, and he lacks the most common skills among us.

Darrovan waded through the group with care, trying not to be intrusive. Guinnian did have a point, he was disturbing them. Who knew how important their work was? Whatever they tinkered with fell well beyond Darrovan's grasp. Most of the scientists were polite and far more proficient with conversations than the lead researcher.

After he stepped away, they went back to work, almost as if they had forgotten him. Females made up the majority of the group—nearly seventy percent. The only other males in the room were young, fresh-faced youths who were more like a teacher's assistant than a full-blown doctor.

Maybe they are. Without crisp degrees, Guinnian can shine all the more.

The professor noted not only their boyish looks and their stature. All were short and diminutive. Guinnian towered over them all despite being a stick-like figure.

Perhaps genetics was the culprit, the weakest taking occupations that required the most intellect. As their species evolved from the hunter-gatherer ancestors, the feeble took roles that bolstered their societal position.

On the other hand, perhaps Guinnian chose them on a subconscious level, packing the team with fertile females and near-impotent .and nonthreatening males. Perhaps Guinnian expressed dominance through this method, which Darrovan found laughable.

While blagrens evolved from great nocturnal hunters, their ancestors roamed in pacts, their strength in numbers. They lacked a common trait of singular dominance among the sothor species—the assertive alpha syndrome boosted other ethnicities or turned detrimental to others.

None of the others from the research team stuck out to him. They were all a blur of names, faces, and scents. Only Guinnian proved unforgettable. Good or ill, he left an impression.

Darrovan wound his way to the back of the room, to the thick transparisteel. Inside, the same white walls and floor stretched out, but in the center, an inky, writhing mass sat. It expanded and contracted, fluctuating like a constant boil of bleak emotions. From the black center, small tendrils of dark lilac arced around the mass, reminding him of contained lightning.

A presence sidled up next to him, and he didn't have to turn to guess it was Guinnian.

"So, what are your thoughts?"

"I don't have the faintest idea yet," Darrovan said honestly. "It's all a little terrifying."

"Nothing? No hypothesis? I would've had a half dozen by now."

Darrovan's brows rose, and he turned to the lead researcher.

The other towered above him by a full head, but without an intimidation factor. Guinnian stood with arms crossed behind his back.

"I just got here, seeing the miasma for the first time. I had, what —ten seconds before you came over, and now I'm supposed to have the answer?"

He rolled his eyes.

"Some of us are not as brilliant as you appear to be."

"Hmm," the other said, twisting his lips. "Rude?"

Darrovan nodded.

"Yeah, a bit."

He shook his head and turned back to the transparisteel. Trepidation washed over him. His heart fluttered in tune with the dynamic miasma.

Without looking, he asked, "Has anyone been back down there since the accident?"

"Accident?"

Darrovan blinked a few times but kept the comments to himself.

"Yes, since Calistor."

"Is that what happened to him?"

The professor gave the other a long look, his brow rising in shock.

"Where do you think he's been?"

Guinnian shrugged.

"I thought he quit."

This brought out a single snort from Darrovan. He nodded with his head.

"Look around. Does this seem like the kind of place you can just quit?"

The lead researcher brought his hands up under his chin, tapping the tips together.

"What do you mean?"

"I think that means you are here to stay."

The professor shook his head, flabbergasted.

"Didn't you know that?"

The look that flashed across Guinnian's face told Darrovan everything he needed. The lead researcher turned on his heel and hurried out of the room.

He's running off to go see Lias.

Darrovan chuckled, imagining what the old man was about to endure, but that suited him just fine. Guinnian could be the old man's problem for the time being.

When Darrovan turned back to the window, he spied a badge reader to the left and ambled over. Below, a large red button sat in its shadow. The label read: Emergency Close.

Well, at least they thought of safety first.

"It won't work," a woman's voice called.

He turned and regarded her for a moment. He gave her a cursory glance, noting her age and shape. Perhaps she was married, and her offspring were guests of the dome?

Darrovan squinted at her, trying to remember her name.

"Kavisha," she supplied.

"Kavisha," he repeated. "Sorry, I must've missed you when I made my rounds. Why won't it work, Kavisha?"

He echoed her name in the hopes of remembering, but he doubted he would. Faces were easy to recall, the names accompanying them, not so much.

"The boss locked it. Won't let anyone through, not even Guinnian."

"Hmm."

He glanced back at the miasma, then the card scanner.

"Are you going to be with us long?"

He tore his eyes away from the badge detector.

"That remains to be seen. Perhaps. What do you do here?"

She gave an awkward smile.

"Nothing of consequence, I'm afraid. Nothing like the others."

Her eyes flickered to the scientists about the room.

For a moment, Darrovan thought her actions seemed skittish, but chalked it up to paranoia. He still didn't trust Lias or the reason why he was here. If what Lias imparted was true, what assurances kept them from taking him out back and shooting him once this was all done?

Another notion tickled his mind. What if the miasma wasn't an alien at all? What if the military made it and brought Darrovan in to see if they could fool him with some form of advanced AI?

"Do you have a family?"

"Hmm?"

Darrovan tore away from those somber thoughts.

"Oh, no. Women are quite the enigma to me. You?"

Kavisha smiled. "Yes, two hatchlings."

He nodded, and his eyes narrowed.

The term hatchlings was antiquated, but she could have come from a puritan family upbringing. It begged the question of why she was here. Generally speaking, most religions frowned on the sciences as blasphemy.

"What do you hope to achieve?" Kavisha asked.

He looked at her, and her eyes darted to the vault beyond.

"Oh."

He pondered the question for a moment. His eyes darted to her chest, and he saw the black badge dangling.

"I guess contact, to converse. It's such a fascinating discovery. I'm hopeful and terrified."

"Terrified? In what way?"

The tips of his claws extended, and he scratched his neck. He fought the urge to yawn. The abduction interrupted his sleep cycle, and he had yet to get some rest.

"In something as monumental as this, there's always the chance something could go wrong."

He waved a hand to the vault.

"If this is something from beyond our world, is this the right environment for such a meeting? What do our initial actions say about us as a species? We've locked it in a vault."

She blinked a few times, her face going lax.

"Oh, never thought of that."

He nodded.

"It doesn't set the best tone. However, there's also the worry of our interstellar guest."

She frowned.

"What do you mean?"

"Who's to say it comes in peace? Perhaps this is a reconnaissance mission, a cursory incursion to the inevitable invasion to harm us."

She shook her head.

"You're paranoid, Professor. Why would you think such things?"

A sigh escaped him as he shook his head.

"Because our history is rife with atrocities. If we're willing to do that to our own, why would another species be any different? Do they see us as vermin or a threat?"

He peered through the transparisteel.

"It's like I said, I'm hopeful and terrified."

She gave a radiant smile.

"That's good; you remain hopeful. It's always fascinating hearing other people's opinions."

Her grin faltered, and she motioned with her head.

"Well, I've got to get back. Thanks for talking; it was insightful."

She strode away, weaving through the scientists with deft feet. She managed not to bump into any of the milling personnel.

Darrovan turned back to the vault and allowed a smile to spread on his face. It was the first conversation he had with a woman that wasn't either presenting an assignment, college paper, or a reprimand.

First Brelo, and now Kavisha. Maybe coming here would change his luck after all.

His eyes flickered back to the badge reader. Should he even try now that he knew it was disabled? He shrugged. He had to, at least once, otherwise, why was he here?

He slapped the card against the wall device.

"Welcome, Professor."

The door hissed and popped outward before sliding along the interior wall.

He searched for Kavisha, but he didn't see her.

Another female who was closer stood with her mouth open. She blinked in shock a few times. Darrovan noticed the other scientist looking up from their work, stopping to gawk. In ones and twos, they left their stations, making their way towards him.

Taking a deep breath, he stepped through the door.

Almost instantly, the door started to slide shut. Perhaps a safety mechanism or a sensor like the vault's front hatch, but Darrovan held the notion that it was meant to keep others from following him.

He heard a startled voice say something, but the door moving drowned it out.

As soon as the door closed and sealed, the room went quiet. The ringing came back, and his breathing sounded like the rush of a waterfall. Beneath that, the thrum from the Dark Portal filled the stillness.

He could feel it, hear it, a deep pulse thrumming in regular intervals, almost like breathing. Slow and deep, a near-steady cadence. Virtually undetectable in the noise was a hiss, the sound of raking nails along a chalkboard but softer.

"Professor!" one of the scientists called through the intercom.

He glanced back.

"You need a hazmat suit! It's not safe."

He shook his head and turned back towards the dark matter. If it intended harm, he doubted a hazmat suit would make a difference.

His insides squirmed.

The room crackled with energy, making his pores tighten.

This might not have been a good idea.

His palms turned damp, and his scales twitched in anxiety. He brushed his hands against his trousers.

Careful steps drew him closer to the miasma. The pitch changed. Instead of deep and soft, it grew higher and louder.

His bowels fluttered.

Please, don't let me shit myself!

He took a few steps away, and the noise receded to its earlier level. Another few steps forward. The volume returned.

What am I doing? Am I toying with a viper? Is it going to strike me like it did Calistor?

He backed off, giving the portal a wide berth. The surface rippled like tiny waves, marring the smooth surface in a wash of ocean-like motion.

How would he even begin to understand or converse? Lias spoke of using placards and colors and calling objects out, but aquatic animals could learn behavior from rote memorization.

No, this had to be more complex. If this was an alien, how did it get here? That meant traveling through the universe, which implied higher intelligence.

The absurdity of how stupid he'd been when approaching this hit him like an anvil. A random notion struck him: to find out what the portal wanted, discovering its intent, the conversation had to start somewhere. A writer friend once said, "you can't edit a blank page." This chance meeting was Darrovan's blank page.

"I don't know if you can understand me," he spoke to the rippling mass, "but I have to assume you're alive."

He felt stupid for speaking aloud, talking to a mass of roiling energy, but how foolish would it be to assume it couldn't detect sounds, speak, or understand?

If this miasma was a natural phenomenon, undoubtedly, the scientists would have already figured it out. If it was a military experiment, the sooner he played along, the sooner he could leave. If he found out a way to explain what it was, giving Lias some answers and direction, could he return to the life ripped from him?

Doubt, with a robust dose of fear, gripped him. Guinnian was right. Darrovan wasn't a scientist. In fact, surrounded by such erudite elites, he was a conspiracy theorist. He might as well play the part, at least until he knew something more.

"I can't begin to quantify what you are or what you want, but I'm not here to hurt you. I'm uh … if you're what I suspect, a genuine life form, you're my life's work. If you're from another world, an alien, you've proven me correct."

Darrovan glanced to the right, noticing the small lecture-like podium with a stool.

Calistor must've set it up before the Dark Portal attacked him.

That thought alone made his throat constrict.

With stiff legs, he ambled over, grabbed the stool, and moved towards the center of the room. Still a healthy distance away, he perched on the seat.

"Perhaps with proof of your existence, I'll no longer be mocked."

He leaned forward, resting elbows along his thighs.

"Everyone always said life out there doesn't exist; we're the only ones."

He shook his head.

"I don't believe that to be true. Mathematical probability dictates as such."

He stood then.

The buzz, the static, he felt earlier grew sharper. His scales quivered under his clothes. Perhaps it was best to cut the first meeting short? If this miasma reacted at all like a cornered animal, it would grow bold and attack. Better to have short intervals until he gained its trust.

He tapped his chest.

"Darrovan. Darrovan."

He watched the surface ripple, shimmering, boiling. The dark lilac tendrils pulsed each time he spoke. He couldn't think of any other word to describe it.

"I'm Darrovan. That's my name."

He patted his torso one last time.

"Darrovan."

He gave a small, tight smile and backed away. He thought about just walking out, but if it was an alien life form, he didn't want to give the wrong impression. Perhaps the gesture would be rude?

Further, he didn't trust the entity yet, not after visiting Calistor. If anything, visiting the catatonic patient gave him a hardy injection of caution.

When he reached the wall, he carded the reader. The door opened and moved to the side.

As he stepped through, the portal hissed in a dark, deep resonance.

"Darrovan."

Chapter 4: The Observatory

Back in the observatory, surrounded by the black floor and dim lights, Lias idly tapped his cane on the floor, Guinnian paced, and Darrovan awaited the other two.

Lias's lips twisted and his eyes were distant. Darrovan couldn't read the older man yet, but he seemed deep in thought.

The professor leaned against a desk, his fingers rubbing along the smooth edge while he watched the other two.

Guinnian prattled on with a petulant voice. It infuriated him that the miasma spoke to what the lead researcher referred to as a nonacademic.

The portal's speech sent a chill down the professor's spine.

No way that was faked. It's got to be real.

The implications twisted his stomach.

Darrovan had to cast aside all doubt on the whole project. This wasn't a military experiment, or a trick of some sort. He wasn't in a cell or being executed. This was authentic.

A freaking alien!

Guinnian turned to him.

"I don't understand what you mean when you say 'spoke.' Where's the proof? Why would it speak to you of all people?"

Darrovan frowned. Why indeed?

"Maybe because I just talked to it, assumed a level of intelligence. An alien implies travel from a distant planet, a level of sophistication we haven't achieved."

He shrugged and shook his head. Guinnian irritated him, and he took the opportunity to jab back.

"Or maybe I didn't poke and prod it."

Guinnian went still, pausing as if an epiphany hit him. Darrovan had noticed this earlier when they spoke down in the vault.

"How else are we supposed to test it?"

The professor shifted on his feet. He didn't care about upsetting Guinnian with facts, he was a scientist after all, but how'd he react to out-of-the-box thinking?

"I'd probably start with the least invasive method. You said you had an ... ethologist. Did you ever think of just watching first?"

"Of course, we thought of that—and we did watch it!"

Vexation etched Guinnian's face.

"The audacity—"

"But did you observe with a clinical eye?" Darrovan interrupted. "I mean, it appears you assumed it wasn't intelligent."

Guinnian waved the question away and turned his attention to Lias.

"This reckless behavior without regard for scientific inquiry's ample reason to remove the professor from the vault."

Lias planted the cane on the floor with a soft thud. Darrovan wasn't sure he heard the sound or imagined it. The old man's fingers fiddled with the globe on the end.

Lias nodded.

"Yes, you're right, it was rather brash."

Darrovan's brow perked up at the words.

Was it that simple? Just reckless behavior on his part, and he'd be sent home? He wondered if the other "guests" knew this, too.

"Then again," Lias continued, eyeing Guinnian, "he made more progress in a five-minute conversation than you did in months."

Guinnian sputtered. Didn't he think Lias would call out his lack of results?

Darrovan suppressed a smile.

Lias sighed, and his eyes darted to Darrovan.

With thick incredulity and a smile, he asked, "A conversation? Really? Where'd you come up with that?"

"You can't be serious," Guinnian protested. "He doesn't know his way around a lab other than what he gleaned from textbooks. The professor put the other scientists at risk."

Lias's expression shifted, something between a smirk and disbelief, and his eyes flickered between the two before settling on the lead researcher.

"It's what he's here for."

Guinnian opened his mouth to continue, but Lias cut him off.

"He proved beyond all doubt that whatever the Dark Portal is, it's intelligent. What have you proved?"

"Miasma. And we proved intelligence long ago!"

"Yes, Guinnian," Lias nodded, "you did, and you haven't let anyone forget, either. I misspoke. You proved its intelligence, but Professor Weiv verified sentience in five-minutes. I'd say he produced more results, wouldn't you?"

"Results? What results? I see no empirical data," the lead researcher said, throwing his arms into the air.

Lias reached into his pocket and pulled out a small remote. He pointed at the far wall, and a screen sputtered to life. Before that,

Darrovan thought it was just an ordinary wall, and the revelation surprised him.

He remembered Talcen's guns in the lobby, hidden behind panels in the ceiling. What else inside the dome appeared to be one thing and not the other? Did he have to scrutinize everything now? What, if anything, was trustworthy? What could he take for real?

The video played, and Darrovan recognized the scene, the last few seconds before he left the room with the Dark Portal.

"Darrovan," the portal hissed.

Guinnian ceased fidgeting and stood as still as stone.

"Strange," he finally said.

"What is?" Darrovan inquired.

He couldn't help himself. Despite Guinnian's inability to articulate thoughts into a proper conversation, ignoring the most brilliant mind in the room wasn't a good idea either.

The lead researcher turned with a languid movement and regarded him. "That you produced such results with your barbaric approach while lacking knowledge in all scientific fields."

Darrovan rolled his eyes. He should've expected that kind of response.

Guinnian shuffled his feet and spoke to Lias.

"I stand corrected. Though rare that I'm wrong, my appraisal remains: the professor's out of his depth, and is a danger to us all."

The old man smiled, but his teeth didn't show, nor did it reach his eyes.

"Yes, you may be correct, but Professor Weiv has a brilliant mind, the same as you, and he approaches things differently. A fresh set of eyes might be what we need. We're behind schedule, and results are expected. It's an accurate assessment to assume that what may be obvious to you, he will be blind to, but the opposite holds true."

Lias tapped the cane twice on the floor.

"Your cautionary objections are noted. From now on, before Professor Weiv enters the room with the Dark Portal—"

"Miasma," Guinnian inserted.

"—the room will be cleared of all other scientists." Lias's gaze danced to Darrovan. "Since I brought you here for the sole purpose of finding out what this thing is, how would you like to proceed?"

"What?" Guinnian interjected. "I'm the lead researcher. I think I should be the one to decide."

Damn, think much of yourself?

Again, Lias gave him that tight, placating smile, and Darrovan suspected it masked a grimace.

"We've tried your way for months. Now, it's someone else's turn."

I wish I could think of something to take the wind out of that bag.

As the sentiment arced through him, a revelation manifested.

"I have a question," Darrovan said, cutting through the building tension.

His eyes locked with the lead researcher.

"If it was your call, how did Calistor get injured?"

Guinnian's back straightened, and he visibly bristled. Darrovan read the indignation flaring through him.

"I'm not responsible for his injuries. I wasn't even there."

He sent a cold look Lias's way.

"And no one bothered to tell me until you mentioned it earlier."

Lias shrugged.

"Honestly, what good would it have done?"

"None," Guinnian answered with his usual less-than-tactful approach. "It would've been a distraction, and we have more important things to focus on. Though, if there are records, I could use that to further our understanding of the miasma."

Whatever goodwill Lias clung to faded at those words.

"Then, let us not distract you anymore. Return to your work."

Guinnian frowned. He started to open his mouth but thought better of it. He turned, paused to glare at Darrovan, then departed.

Once the elevator shut, Darrovan turned to Lias.

"Has anyone ever told him that he's an asshole?"

Lias chuckled.

"Not to my knowledge."

"Well, someone should."

"Are you offering, Professor?"

Darrovan debated for a moment, then sighed.

"It may end up slipping out."

This brought another chuckle from the old man.

"I'm sure there are better things for you to talk about than him. Now that you've seen the Dark Portal for yourself, what's on your mind, Professor?"

Darrovan turned to the left, noting the military-aligned chairs tucked under the desks, and ambled over. He pulled one out and offered one to Lias before taking one for himself.

Once seated, Darrovan blew out a breath.

Might as well get the big question out of the way first.

"I can't just leave, can I?"

Lias shook his head.

"No, not now. Even if I wanted to let you, others wouldn't allow a premature departure."

"Now? Does this mean that later down the road?"

A nod.

The tension in his chest eased.

Well, that's something.

"My release is contingent upon figuring out the Dark Portal." It wasn't a question.

Another slow nod. "The simple answer is yes."

"Well, what's the not-so-simple answer?"

"Everything's contingent upon the Dark Portal. Up until now, we didn't know for sure it was sentient, or had the capability to learn."

"But I thought you said—"

"Yes, the cards. We tested for intelligence, not sentience. Besides, there are aquatic species in captivity that can do that. They're able to point out cards as you call them, yet they lack speech."

"So, you're basing the assumption of sentience on the intelligence to speak. Animals communicate with one another."

"But not with us. Yes, the assumption's based upon higher intelligence."

Darrovan leaned back, letting the weight of the words and reality set in. He was pulled—no, ripped from his life, and now this dome would be his new, indefinite home. A bleak future, sure, but it could've been much worse.

Not long ago, he thought he was headed for a dark, cold cell, or worse, the gallows. Being alive and free to study the first possible alien life form was too exciting to stay angry about. Being part of the most profound discovery in their history required sacrifices. If a few minor inconveniences like missing favorite shows and eating TV dinners were the worst, how could he complain? What did any of that matter against the opportunity to converse with another life form not of their planet?

"How long?" he asked the old man.

Lias blinked a few times and frowned.

"How long what?"

"How long do you want me to stay?"

"I don't want you to stay any longer than necessary, but I can assure you that you won't leave until a satisfactory resolution is reached. Afterward, I don't see why you couldn't return to your life on the outside."

He hesitated for a moment.

"You will, of course, have to sign nondisclosure agreements and be subjected to random military probes into your social life, but your day-to-day activities will go unhindered."

Darrovan's gaze flickered up to the short man sitting opposite of him. What he said hadn't bothered him nearly as much as the tone. While gentle, it left no room for negotiation, and he got an inkling of how limited Lias's authority really was beyond the confines of the dome.

His heart fluttered, rising into his throat. Darrovan realized his initial assessment had been correct. He *was* a prisoner. The only difference now was the lack of physical chains, but the proverbial noose tightened around his neck all the same.

"Define what you consider done."

"When we have a definitive understanding and dialogue between the Dark Portal and us, and we've learned all we can, and there's no ill-intent. We need to know what it is, where it came from, why it's here, and, more importantly, if it means us harm."

The last words rankled him.

"I can answer that for you," Darrovan said. "Yes, of course, it means us harm."

Lias leaned back in the chair, his face full of uncertainty. He rolled the cane in his fingers.

"Okay, I'll bite. How did you come to that conclusion?"

"Do I know for certain? No, but the notion hit me during the visit earlier. Our primal ancestors could track their quarry down and corner it. When prey's backed up against the wall, they do two things, run or fight. I believe the Dark Portal may be cornered with nowhere to run. Calistor got too close, and it lashed out."

A small grin reached Lias's lips.

"Are you an authority on evolution now, Professor?"

He sidestepped the question and continued.

"What if we're looking at this all wrong? What if the Dark Portal isn't a prey but a predator? What if this is the beginning of an onslaught, an invasion? Maybe it's a reconnaissance. Perhaps it's come to learn our capabilities and weaknesses? How can we be certain it won't strike once it's aware?"

Darrovan sighed.

"What's to keep us from being destroyed?"

Lias ran his fingers through his wispy beard. When he finally spoke, his voice was soft and quiet.

"You're not the first person to think such things."

The admission made him feel better.

"Who was the first?"

"Me."

A grin spread across the professor's face, and he took a deep breath.

"Glad I'm not the only one who's paranoid."

"Paranoia, Professor, will keep you alive. Carelessness will get you and others killed."

Lias's voice turned weary, and a sadness glimmered in his eyes.

"Calistor was … a touch overzealous in his hunger to learn. The moment you don't respect what you don't understand, you end up dead."

Darrovan couldn't help nodding in agreement. An old classmate from college, who took a commission in the military as an engineer came to mind, and imparted cautionary tales that Darrovan took to heart.

"A demolition expert knows their craft inside and out, yet accidents happen, and people die."

Darrovan relayed the words to the old man.

"Yes, but in that case, it's carelessness," Lias said. "Surety of knowledge leads to calamitous results. In many ways, that's why I'm glad you're here. Theory's one thing, but being faced with a real alien is quite different."

Lias cocked his head to the side, and his fingers fell away from his facial hair.

"How do you propose we proceed with this potential enemy?"

"Well, before we assume beyond all doubt that it is, we must proceed with utmost goodwill. Perhaps it's nothing more than an alien race trying to make contact. Maybe they discovered us and came to share knowledge, introduce themselves to their celestial neighbors."

Lias's eyes narrowed.

"You seem a bit indecisive on how to treat it, Professor."

"We can't know for certain until it happens, but we can take precautions."

"Such as?"

He blew out a deep breath.

He'd had time to think about this—not only down in the vault before meeting the alien, but on the elevator ride back up and enduring Guinnian's rants.

"I'd say first we block the transparisteel in the vault. Use blackout curtains or boards, anything to block the view. Let's assume for a moment that the Dark Portal possesses the same capabilities we do. One of those is vision. We must protect ourselves and limit its capacity from seeing further into the vault.

"We must also assume this … entity can hear, especially since it spoke my name. So, audio and speech. We need to make sure it can't hear any more than what's necessary, so remove any kind of communication devices from the wall. Without the ability to confirm the miasma's capabilities, we can't ascertain whether it can access our electronics and eavesdrop."

He paused.

"Since you recorded my session with the alien, I'd leave the cameras for posterity, but I wouldn't make it known."

Lias nodded. "So, spying on it without its knowledge? Limit its ability to glean knowledge from its surroundings. Anything else?"

"You've already locked down the other scientists from reaching it, and I think that's a good measure, but we should isolate Calistor as well."

Lias blinked a few times, his head twitching at the words. Several expressions rippled across his leathery visage, most notably, his eyes misted over. When he spoke, his voice remained soft, but there was a tightness.

"What does my nephew have to do with the portal?"

"Well," Darrovan started, trying to figure out how to not make an ass out of himself like Guinnian did. "Can you tell me beyond all doubt that he *is* still Calistor?"

"You think he may be contaminated, like a disease, or worried about being controlled?"

Darrovan paused, and Brelo's image materialized in his mind.

"Either possibility's too great to ignore. We've got doctors up there on the medical wing, and we should limit the chance."

"If diseased, why isn't the medical team sick?"

He shook his head and shrugged. This was all beyond his depth. In fields of study like physics and medicine, he grasped the subjects like water slipping through fingers.

"Perhaps it's not an airborne sickness. How do we know for certain that a part of the Dark Portal isn't inside him, learning about us while Calistor's catatonic?"

Lias nodded, and suddenly weariness washed through his features. He rubbed his eyes.

"Perhaps you're right. We'll take measures to ensure its inability to learn from us in the future and limit interactions to only what's necessary. There are plenty of rooms. We'll isolate him. Anything else?"

Relief shot through him. He had hoped Lias wouldn't become defensive and think he was overreacting. But now, he had to speak the truth, no matter how uncomfortable it might be.

"Yes." He grimaced. "I don't know how to put this…"

"Perhaps bluntly, Professor?"

His eyes met the old man's gaze.

"I had an urge."

Lias's brow twitched up, and a wolfish smile stole across him.

"Indeed? What's her name? This may become uncomfortable for me if you say my daughter."

"No," Darrovan said, frowning.

He stood and paced.

"I'm being serious."

Lias's smile faded, and he held up his arms, gesturing for him to continue.

"During my visit with Calistor earlier, I had an urge to …"

"Unplug the machine?" the director finished, his voice full of an emotion Darrovan couldn't pinpoint. The old man's gaze was on a distant patch of floor.

"Yes," he breathed.

Lias nodded, tugging on his wispy facial hair.

"You aren't the only one. I had the urge as well. So did Dr. Brelo. At first, I thought the notion came from sympathy, a mercy killing."

His eyes darted up.

"But now, it might be something more."

Darrovan shivered.

Could the alien have found some way to influence them? Could they fight the implanted suggestions? Was what they experienced the limit of those capabilities? What would happen if the impulses grew stronger?

A weighted silence stretched between both men, neither voicing the dark path their thoughts hurled down.

"Anything else?" Lias asked.

Darrovan shook his head.

"Not at this time. Those are only my initial thoughts."

Lias stood.

"Well, it seems you have your work cut out for you, Professor. Best not delay. Take the rest of the day off and approach this tomorrow when you're rested. I'll send all the files down to your room. You can review them and get caught up."

Chapter 5: The Voice in the Dark

Darrovan?

Darrovan!

Darrovan's eyes snapped open. He jerked, and the folder lying on his chest slid to the floor.

Did he dream the portal called to him?

Still lying on his back, he rubbed his eyes. Maybe he was just tired … or going crazy.

Darrovan.

A lump formed in his throat.

It wasn't a dream. The alien called to him. How? His room was ten levels above the vault. He shouldn't be able to hear the voice, but it beckoned to him in his sleep, and that meant it could only be in his mind.

In a moment of terror, he realized that if the miasma called to him with telepathy, then Calistor in the infirmary might be just as susceptible.

He jerked upright, and the remaining papers lying beside him clattered to the floor. His eyes tracked down to the disarray. Angry red classification markings stared back up at him. Words like Top Secret, Classified, Non-Releasable, and No Civilians screamed out in bold. Finer print in black itemized the possible penalties. The military didn't even try to hide the blacklisting, imprisonment, or execution. If anyone this deep in the facility didn't realize all the expectations and implications of their job or requirements, they had to be dense. Guinnian came to mind.

Darrovan.

If the portal reached into his mind, perhaps all his thoughts were laid bare?

He tested the theory.

Can you hear me?

When no response came, he breathed easier. Another unsettling idea jabbed at him. Perhaps it feigned ignorance? Or maybe the miasma lacked understanding?

Biesh gul, Darrovan.

What the hell was that? An alien word?

Come here, Darrovan.

Heat constricted his chest, and the scales on the side of his neck quivered.

The portal was learning, either that or projecting its language into Darrovan's mind. This proved sentience at the very least, a higher cognitive capacity. Guinnian would be happy, but a chill ran down Darrovan's spine.

This wasn't good. Not on the second day.

Yes, he expected to make some headway and hopefully turn over the project to Lias, but it happened all too fast. Either the alien life form duped them all, or it still learned despite the curbing measures put in place. And the only way it could be learning …

Oh, shit, Calistor!

Darrovan rolled out of bed, feet shuffling over the forgotten papers, and hurried to put his uniform on. He glanced at the chrono on the nightstand. One-twenty-seven in the morning. Did the time have any significance? Most would be asleep, but the vault had round-the-clock workers.

He pushed the call button on the intercom, paging the vault.

"Kavisha, here."

Darrovan frowned.

What was she doing awake? Hadn't he met her this morning?

Then, he remembered.

They had come for him in the dead of night, and when he arrived, it would have been during her shift.

"Kavisha, it's Darrovan."

"Professor?"

"Yeah, anything happening down there right now? Anything strange?"

Silence followed for a moment.

"No, nothing, no one here but me. Something wrong?"

He frowned.

She should be able to see something!

Then, it clicked. They blocked the windows to the vault's inner chamber, where the miasma resided.

Is this why it's calling out? Because it cannot see or hear anything anymore?

"Uh, no," he stammered. "Just checking in to see if the time of day had any effects on the portal."

She paused, and he imagined her scanning the room behind her. Her voice came back uncertain.

"Nothing's different."

"Okay. Thank you, Kavisha."

He clicked off the comm device.

That left Calistor.

He doubted they placed round-the-clock surveillance other than monitors. He lay catatonic, and they moved him to a secured room.

Grabbing the black badge, he clipped it to his shirt and stepped out into the hallway.

He reached the elevators and pushed the fourth button, descending one floor. Darrovan thought of calling Talcen—or whoever was on watch—but decided against it. What if he reached Calistor's room and nothing was amiss? That would waste the guard's time, not to mention making him feel stupid.

The doors parted, and he stepped out.

The infirmary stood dark with a crypt-like silence.

A disquiet lanced him.

The only light coming from within radiated from the yellow tubes running across the top of the walls and small fluorescents mounted under the foyer's medicine cabinets.

He glanced left, down the curving hallway, but headed right, passing several doors with darkened windows.

Darrovan. Biesh. Biesh gul, Darrovan.

The professor's steps faltered.

The voice.

He closed his eyes, blocking out the summoning. The portal had awoken him, and in a groggy state, he missed an important detail. Whenever the alien called, an underlying impulse accompanied it. A mental tug tickled his mind. The words reverberated in his head, and he wanted to obey the call.

"No," the professor said aloud. "You don't control me."

Hei rah sendul preshka?

"No, I don't know what you're saying."

He shook his head, eyes closed tight.

"Get out of my head."

The portal went silent for a moment, and Darrovan noted a presence that faded with the retreat. Almost without warning, it returned. The intense flood battered against his mind.

BIESH GUL, DARROVAN.

"NO!" he screamed, dropping to his knees.

The cold floor seeped through the trousers. He clutched his head.

"Get out!"

He rocked back and forth, fighting against the onslaught.

The compulsion to obey tore through him. His insides tightened. He felt sick. Whatever the alien wanted, it couldn't be good, not with it abandoning all sense of decorum. Compulsion, a sense of obedience, festered within him.

Why would the portal need him to obey? It couldn't win, couldn't control him. The wrongness left an ache in him.

The conversation with Lias shot through his mind, the notion that the miasma meant them harm. If he was unsure before, he wasn't now. Maybe it was the only way it could communicate, but a mental invasion didn't bode well. If it can take control of them, what kept it from doing so?

The intensity of the presence faded but still lingered.

Biesh. Biesh gul, Calistor.

The blood drained from Darrovan's face, and his mouth fell open.

Oh, God!

A plume of cold raced down his spine. If the presence called and controlled Calistor, Lias's young nephew would act as a proxy, giving a compliant body to the extraterrestrial.

The professor lurched to his feet, rushing down the hall. Calistor's room loomed at the end, one they deemed the furthest from the central chamber. There was no chance of him overhearing, sensing, or learning while unconscious.

Darrovan bolted to the door and peered through the glass pane.

Calistor stood against the far wall. His body trembled.

Goosebumps tightened between Darrovan's scales. A spike of dread stabbed his chest.

Calistor was a helpless pawn. He had to save him. Slapping the black badge against the reader, the door opened.

"Calistor," he called in a soft voice. As a professor of alien theory, medical conditions were beyond him. Still, he'd heard stories of those who sleepwalked, and how they reacted once awakened. He didn't want to spook him.

"Calistor?"

The younger sothor turned towards the sound, and dread filled the professor.

Calistor's eyes were open and glossed over, but the pupils were small, almost nonexistent.

Without warning, Calistor sprang forward. Claws sprang out as the patient attacked. An otherworldly bellow tore from his throat.

The two bodies collided. Air rushed out of Darrovan as they tumbled to the floor. Calistor slashed at him.

In the frantic tangle of flailing extremities, Darrovan managed to trap the arms. Calistor jerked, trying to free himself without success. Then, he went still as if in thought.

His mouth opened. Needle-sharp teeth gleamed with saliva.

"Oh, shit!"

In a flash, Calistor lurched forward and sank into Darrovan's left shoulder. Serrated canines pierced flesh.

Darrovan screamed.

Pain shot through him. His shoulder flashed both hot and cold. Calistor pulled back, small chunks of cloth and flesh came free. Blood dripped from his mouth and splattered down the front of his shirt.

He opened wide again, moving for a second bite when blue-white light arced out. The energy hit him square in the chest, and Calistor toppled backward.

Darrovan twisted, searching down the hallway. Talcen stood with blaster raised. A wisp of faint smoke curled from the end.

The nozzle drifted over to him.

"No, don't shoot!"

"What are you doing, Professor?" Talcen's crisp voice asked. Darrovan remembered that tone upon exiting the main elevator the first time.

Was that just yesterday or this morning? The days are blurring together.

"Why are you out of your bed, Professor?"

Confusion ripped through Darrovan.

What did this have to do with anything?

But he dismissed it as he struggled to free himself from underneath Calistor's unconscious body. His weak left arm and shoulder ached with pain and lay useless.

"Help me."

Talcen waited a moment, deciding. Without holstering the weapon, he stepped forward and reached out with a free hand. Darrovan grabbed hold, and Talcen pulled him free with ease.

Damn, he's strong.

Once out from under Calistor, Darrovan rose to his knees. Talcen loomed over him.

"I asked you a question. Why are you out of your quarters, Professor?"

Darrovan shook his head.

"You wouldn't understand."

The barrel shifted and squared on his chest.

"Try me."

He blinked and sputtered, eyeing the gray badge on Talcen's chest.

"But—but—I can't, you're not authorized."

49

He glanced around the hall, seeing the yellow tubes illuminated.

"This isn't a safe area."

Beyond Talcen, the soft whisper of the elevator doors opened, and Sheedah came dashing down the hall with Lias hobbling behind her. Sheedah's eyes widened when she noted the blood oozing through Darrovan's shirt.

"Professor!"

She faltered, her gaze flickering to her cousin.

"Calistor!"

She rushed to help him.

Lias stepped around Talcen and frowned down at him. Without a word, he hobbled over to the wall and pushed the intercom.

"Brelo?"

After a few moments, the woman's voice answered.

"I'm here, Lias."

"Come down to the infirmary, please? There's been a medical situation."

"Coming."

Lias turned back.

"Are you in pain?"

Darrovan tried to shrug and winced.

"Yes, but he didn't bite through bone."

Lias's brows rose in surprise.

"He bit you? Calistor's catatonic."

"No," Talcen cut in, "he isn't. I had to stun him to get him off Professor Weiv."

Lias rubbed his chin, the wispy strains growing there.

"Really?"

"Yes."

Darrovan frowned and scrutinized Talcen.

"Hang on. How did you even know I was here or in trouble?"

"I monitor the hall sensors. I detected an open door in your quarters and the elevator in motion. I came to investigate why you'd be in the infirmary at this hour."

"You're spying on me?"

Talcen's visor centered on him.

"Yes."

Lias shook his head.

"No, he isn't. He watches everyone."

Darrovan eyed Lias.

"How did you know to come?"

"I called him," Talcen supplied. "That's my duty."

Lias nodded, and for the first time, the old man noted Talcen's blaster still pointed at Darrovan. He tapped the sentry's arm.

"Put away your blaster and return to your post."

"He still hasn't answered my questions," Talcen protested.

Lias took a deep breath.

"He'll answer mine. Go on."

In a fluid motion, Talcen holstered the weapon, turned on his heel, and left. As the guard made the elevator, the doors parted, and a woman exited. A wave of ease washed over Darrovan.

Despite the terror that just occurred, the doctor's presence soothed the remaining worry.

Still, their first encounter started off rockier than Darrovan would have liked. She didn't like being told to leave the infirmary.

Lias glanced down at him.

"Can you stand, Professor?"

He pulled his eyes away from Brelo, nodded, and rose, grimacing as he clutched the wounded arm close.

Inside the medical bay, the doctor cut the shirt free and cleaned the wound.

Lias stirred. "What happened, Professor?"

"I can't say."

"Can't or won't?"

"The doctor and your—" he almost said daughter "—assistant don't have clearance."

Lias paled, and his neck scales rippled.

"Indeed. That's most distressing."

The old man of the dome waited until the doctor finished and gave a shot of pain reliever and antibiotics. He instructed her to restrain Calistor in the bed, this time with cuffs and a straight jacket. When she completed the task, he thanked her and excused both Sheedah and Brelo. Once the women had left, Lias turned a critical eye to him.

Darrovan began without prompting.

"The portal can speak to me. I heard it."

"How?"

"I don't know. I was asleep when it called to me."

"I thought you had to be present."

"So did I."

"And the call woke you up?"

"Yes. At first, I thought it a dream, but it called to me again."

"Is that it?"

51

Darrovan shook his head.

"No, it said something else, something in its language. Then, repeated it again, but in ours. It said, 'Come here, Darrovan.'"

"And did you go?"

"No!"

"What brought you here?"

"I started thinking. I haven't taught the miasma any words, any way to communicate other than my name. If it's learning and can speak to me while I'm unconscious…"

Lias turned in the direction of Calistor's room.

"Who knows who else it's communicating with."

"Precisely."

"So, naturally, you thought of Calistor."

Darrovan nodded.

"What if the Dark Portal didn't attack Calistor?"

Lias padded a few steps away, his back to Darrovan, taking a moment to mull over the implications.

"What if the portal is trying to quicken its learning?"

"Yes."

Lias faced him.

"And Calistor?" he said, jerking in the direction of his nephew.

"I came down to see if there was any change in his state. He was standing in the room. When he turned around … his eyes. You should've seen them."

Darrovan summarized the rest of the story, even relayed the impulse to obey the Dark Portal's command, and Lias stood quiet as he listened to the subsequent attack and rescue.

"You should thank Talcen."

"Talcen shouldn't be spying on me, or anyone for that matter."

Lias gave a tight smile.

"Talcen doesn't spy; he follows orders."

He held up a hand to stave off the impending interruption.

"No, they didn't come from me. As a military member, he's charged with the safety of this facility and its crew. His orders come from superior officers. His only standing order other than the safety of personnel and property is to obey my orders, and no one else's."

Darrovan shook his head in disbelief.

"That's dangerous."

"Why? Because I'm a lunatic?"

"That's not what I meant."

Lias nodded.

"I know. Well," he cleared his throat, "this proves the importance of establishing communication, and we need it quickly. Find out what the hell it wants, why it's here, and what its intentions are."

Darrovan rolled his eyes.

"I've already told you it means us ill. What's it going to take for you to believe me?"

Lias clicked his tongue against his cheek.

"A little bit more, I'm afraid. Trust me, I'm not ignoring your worries. They're valid, but I cannot agree with you if it can be chalked up to miscommunication. We must have unequivocal proof."

He sighed.

"Get some rest. Start first thing in the morning."

Disheartened that the overseer didn't heed his advice, he left the infirmary and headed to his quarters.

In his room, he curled up in bed. As he drifted off to sleep, the Dark Portal called to him, but the impulse to obey was held at bay.

Biesh. Biesh gul, Darrovan. Come.

Chapter 6: What's Your Name?

The lights flickered overhead.

Darrovan paused mid-bite.

His eyes turned upward, watching the bulbs sputter for a few moments.

"Don't worry," Lias said without preamble.

The old man met him in the cafeteria for breakfast the morning after the incident in the medical wing. He sat opposite Darrovan.

"It's just the cycling between commercial power and the generators."

He took another bite and swallowed.

"It does this every few days or so when the solar energy reserves are full. In a couple of hours, they'll flicker again, and we'll be back to regular power."

Darrovan finished chewing. He glanced about the cafeteria, noting the few others within. They didn't appear bothered, no doubt accustomed to the nuances of the dome.

"Are you sure?"

Lias nodded, scooping up another pile on the fork.

"Don't go looking for omens where none are to be found."

Darrovan shook his head but held his tongue.

"How's the bite?"

The professor rotated his left arm.

"Still hurts. Itches like crazy. He took out a few chunks, you know?"

"Be glad Brelo's a maestro at her profession. You might go see her, for more pain meds and antibiotics, of course."

Darrovan glanced at him, his eyes narrowing. Lias pointed at him with the fork.

"Don't need you getting an infection."

Darrovan's eyes flitted around the cafeteria, making sure none were close enough to overhear.

"Doesn't anything from last night bother you?"

Lias took a deep breath.

"You mean this morning? Of course. This whole ordeal does. We're sitting on the greatest discovery of the universe. Or the worst. It's a bomb waiting to go off, but what type remains to be seen."

"I've never known a bomb going off to be a good thing. Shouldn't we be telling the outside world?"

Lias put the fork down.

"Everyone who needs to know does."

The lights flickered again, and Darrovan gazed up, a seed of worry budding in his chest.

"Relax, Professor. Not everything can be attributed to … well, you know."

The old man stood, reaching for the cane.

"I'll be watching during the session."

He ambled away with the tray in one hand and leaning on the cane in the other. Darrovan watched him go for a moment, then his eyes drifted to the floor. A dark blue linoleum stretched the breadth of the room and reminded him of standing water.

At least it breaks up the monotony of white everywhere.

Darrovan glanced down at his plate. He hardly touched the food. Too many factors weighed on him, and the stress robbed him of sleep and appetite.

Lias departed through the door when Darrovan rose. He wouldn't be eating. His assignment awaited, and he couldn't put the task off forever. The sooner he found answers, the sooner he could leave.

The dagger of uncertainty festered like his injured shoulder. Would he be able to return to his life? He doubted it. The knowledge he gained from being here would change him forever. And what story could cover up the truth of the bite marks on his shoulder once healed?

Could he tell the truth that someone bit him? He'd probably have to sign an NDA upon leaving. If the military ever found him in breach of trust … he could guess at what fate awaited him.

The expressionless visor of Talcen came to mind, as did the unwavering blaster pointed at him last night.

At the backbone of the whole operation, a constant reminder of the military presence lingered. Lias may be in charge of the civilians, and Talcen obeyed his orders, but he didn't doubt the military had another agenda in the event of a catastrophe.

Or the release of workers.

He imagined ascending in the main lift only to be shot in the back by Talcen.

Does anyone really leave this place?

Darrovan placed the plate in the receptacle slot. A robotic arm reached out with its clamps and snagged the plate away. Beyond, the buzz of machinery, grills, and dishwashers created a swirl of noise.

Exiting the cafeteria, he turned left and headed for the lift. The soft golden glow within greeted him. Inside, he scanned the badge and pressed the thirteenth floor. His gut tightened as he descended, but whether due to the motion or growing anxiety, he couldn't tell.

Lias suggested a visit to Dr. Brelo, and he would, but he'd use the excuse to leave the miasma if necessary.

The doors parted and deposited him in front of the massive vault door. He scanned the badge again, and it hissed open. Stepping in, he expected to find someone else working, but the room stood empty.

The growing knot in his stomach tightened.

His eyes found the glass panels in the back, all covered with black cloth. Again, the lights fluttered overhead, and the swell of dread rose with his heartbeat.

I'm not a coward, but this doesn't seem like a good idea.

He pushed the thoughts away and exhaled through his nose. The scariest moments in life paled to stepping back into the room with the Dark Portal. Though, to be fair, last night with Calistor came in a close second.

Darrovan, the portal called, almost like a purr.

"Yeah, I'm here," he said to himself.

I know.

His heart fluttered.

The miasma learned new words.

His chest tightened at the thought.

Calistor was the only explanation, unless someone snuck in to commune with the alien. The notion filled him with dread. If that was the case, someone was either being careless or borderline obstructionist. Either thought didn't bode well. Perhaps a mole hid amongst them, a dissenter?

He huffed a breath and continued forward, winding his way to the back. At the badge reader, he stopped at the last barrier before stepping in.

Initially, the idea of conversing with an actual alien thrilled him, but now, disquiet sat in its place. Perhaps he was too judgmental? How would he react if the roles were reversed?

Despite misgivings, he acknowledged the bias and fear. He'd give the miasma another try before determining its level of hostility.

He fumbled for the security placard with sweaty fingers and held it to the reader.

"Welcome, Professor."

The door hissed and popped out like before, sliding along the interior wall.

He stepped in.

In the center of the room, the miasma shimmered. The surface boiled in little waves.

His throat constricted.

The door slid shut behind him, the locks clanking into place.

The quiet room droned with a sound of its own: nothing. Inhaling thundered like a storm. The eerie thrum of the portal reverberated in his torso, rhythmic like a feline.

With stiff legs, he moved to the stool. This time, as he drew near, the pulse didn't change but remained steady. A flow of emotions rippled through him—anxiety, agitation, fear, anger, curiosity, and disdain.

After a moment, Darrovan realized not all those emotions were his.

But which is which?

He sat.

For a long moment, he said nothing, just listened to the slow and deep cadence of the portal. It still reminded him of breathing. Perhaps it was.

And the static hissing beneath, grating like metal against stone, raced down his spine. His teeth ached when he acknowledged the noise, so he tried to block it out.

"Darrovan," the portal hissed in its deep resonance.

He fought the urge to bolt from the room.

"Yes, I'm here."

"Finally."

Darrovan's eyes narrowed, a disturbing thought coming to him.

"You can understand me, can't you?"

"Yes."

"Everything I say?"

"Yes."

The professor rubbed the inside of his legs, drying the sweat from his hands.

"Everything I think?"

No answer.

"How?"

"Calistor."

"Did you hurt him?"

"Pain is temporary; knowledge is forever."

"Who gains knowledge? You or him?"

A brief hesitation.

"Both."

An itch on his jaw flared up, and Darrovan scratched, taking the time to think.

"Okay, let's start with something simple. What's your name?"

"Deh la noss Enu Brek Zhiem-la-dur."

Darrovan blinked a few times.

"Is that your full name or—"

"Zhiem-la-dur."

"Okay," Darrovan said, holding up his hands. "Zhiem-la-dur."

He waited for a few moments, watching the rippling mass before him.

"That's hard to pronounce for me. How about something shorter, simpler? How about ... Lahdur?"

The miasma didn't answer. The surface roiled faster for a moment, then returned to its original state. A sense of agitation flared in Darrovan, and he knew where it originated.

Is that disagreement?

"No?"

Darrovan cocked his head, thinking. He sounded out the elements of the words the portal said, the ones he could remember anyway.

"Zheem lah duhr ... How about Zhidur?"

"Yes, Zhidur."

A held breath escaped him.

"Good, Zhidur."

"Bring me Calistor."

The demand caught him off guard.

"What?"

"Bring me Calistor."

The only question that came to mind, he blurted.

"Why?"

"Translation."

"Calistor is ... in no fit state to speak."

He shifted on the seat, hoping to steer the miasma from its request.

"Where are you from?"

"Away."

A single stifled chuck rose from the professor.

"Where's away?"

"Far."

"Tell me."

Again, the agitation flared within him but stronger, and heat rushed across his belly.

Is that the portal, or is some from me?

A dark tendril reached out from the portal, forming slowly. It stretched the expanse between them.

"Touch."

"Uh, no."

Darrovan shook his head.

"You hurt Calistor the last time."

"Touch."

Darrovan stood, backing away.

The tendril followed.

"You'll hurt me, and then no one will talk to you."

The tendril pulled back, hesitant.

"No pain. Touch. Trust."

"Why?"

"Show you my home. Only you. No one else."

Darrovan hesitated.

"If you hurt me, no one else will come. Do you understand?"

"Yes."

"You'll be alone."

"I already am."

The answer wasn't one he expected.

Did Zhidur mean figuratively? Was it alienated by being here, which only begged the question of how it got here? But Darrovan wouldn't ever know unless he learned all he could.

Touching the tendril wasn't something he wanted to do, and Zhidur seemed to sense this, keeping the tendril back.

"Only us?" Zhidur asked.

Darrovan nodded. "Yes, it's only us."

The unease tightened in his chest. Every logical reason screamed at him not to do as the roiling cloud wanted, but Lias also made the objective clear—he wouldn't leave unless they had answers.

Even if they cost you your life?

"Touch," Zhidur said. "No pain. Only us. Trust."

Darrovan's hand twitched upward, but self-preservation made him stop.

The tendril raced forward, latching onto his arm.

His mind exploded with images.

So much darkness, racing across the void of space. A glitter of stars flashed by. Three moons and two suns exploded into view.

A world filled his mind.

Oceans and continents, great and terrible creatures on land and in the air. Hairless mammals walked on two legs. Monsters on the world carried similar traits to his race but far more massive.

And then nothing.

The tendril released him in a blink of the eye. He fell to his hands and knees.

"Professor!" Lias's voice yelled over the speaker. "Professor? Can you hear me?"

"Yes," Darrovan wheezed.

"Are you alright?"

Darrovan nodded, not trusting his voice. He knew Lias watched through the cameras.

"Spy!" Zhidur hissed.

Darrovan glanced up.

The surface roiled with agitation.

Fury swept through Darrovan, coming from the portal.

"No," he tried to say, to soothe the alien.

"Spy! Deceit! Lies!"

A wave of malice washed through him, more powerful than he ever felt before.

He crumbled to the ground.

A gurgling sound reached his ears. What was it? Where did it come from? Through the fog of emotions, he realized. It was the sound of Lias choking.

How's that possible?

"Stop," the weak voice of the old man came through the speakers.

"Lies!"

Darrovan rose to his knees again.

The miasma fluctuated, boiling like the surface of a storm sweeping across the ocean. Waves of dark energy swirled.

"Help," Lias croaked.

"LIES!"

The malice Darrovan felt earlier intensified, coming to a point.

Two things happened at once.

The lights shut off, plunging the vault into darkness, and the sound of breaking bone and cartilage echoed overhead.

Klaxons rang through the dome.

[LOCKDOWN IN EFFECT] a female, automated voice said over the PA system.

Red light flooded the vault. The vault door hissed open.

Darrovan darted for the hatch.

The sense of being followed arced through him.

Once through, he turned. Zhidur moved, the roiling miasma coming for the door. Darrovan rushed for the badge reader, swiping the black card.

"Close, damn you."

The door, which had already been sliding closed, reversed course. "What the hell? No, close!"

He spied the large red button and the placard: Emergency Close.

He smashed his fist against it.

The hatch slammed shut, rolling forward.

The deafening sound of metal on metal rang through his ears. The impact reverberated through his chest. Glass vials on countertops rattled and fell to the floor.

In the red light, the chamber glowed with a sinister setting.

He scrambled back.

DARROVAN!

I've got to get the hell out of here!

He ran for the elevator.

DARROVAN!

Hell no!

You deceived me! You lied! Only us!

"No, I didn't!"

He made the elevator.

The doors couldn't open fast enough. He swiped the badge and smashed the lobby button. He couldn't stay here. No one should. They had to get out, regroup, and find a way to exterminate the alien.

The elevator ascended.

Chapter 7: Lockdown in Effect

The doors parted, and the red sheen flooded in.

Darrovan bolted from the lift, turning to the left and racing down the hallway. The doors at the end opened as he neared.

In the main auditorium, the bubbling fountain greeted him. Within the saturation of crimson light, the spewing water invoked a mental picture of erupting lava. Red reminded him of violence.

Rage.

[LOCKDOWN IN EFFECT] the automated female voice said.

"I caught it the first time!"

Darrovan didn't stop.

He turned right and raced down the long stretch. His lungs burned.

The single elevator to take him to safety lay ahead. Only the desk of the military member adorned the room. A figure stepped into view, another faceless sentry.

"Halt," the familiar voice said.

Darrovan skidded to a stop, his legs aching. "Talcen?"

"Who else, Professor?"

His hand dropped by his blaster.

"Where are you going?"

He pointed to the elevator.

"Out! We've got to get out."

"You aren't going anywhere."

He waved a hand around.

"Didn't you notice the red lights? Hear the voice? We're on lockdown. No one comes in, no one goes out."

"Are you mad? We've got to escape while we can. The—the—"

He stopped himself. What could he say? He wasn't supposed to reveal anything to anyone.

"There's no reason to panic."

[LOCKDOWN IN EFFECT]

Sweat poured down his back.

Then, Darrovan remembered the sickening crunch of bone through the speakers.

He gulped. "Lias is dead."

Talcen drew his blaster in a smooth motion.

"What did you say?"

"Lias is dead."

The nozzle came up. Darrovan raised his hands.

"I didn't do it!"

"Then, how did you come to the conclusion he's—"

"I overheard through the speakers."

"You overheard through the speakers?"

Each word came slow, and when Talcen said it like that, it sounded ludicrous.

"We're in danger!"

"From what? Nothing can reach us down here."

Darrovan grabbed him by the tunic. Didn't he see?

"It's already down here, you fool!"

Pain blossomed on the side of his face and in his knees. Stars plumed in his vision. A moment later, he realized what transpired. Talcen had struck him, and Darrovan fell to the floor.

"What—?"

"Talcen!" Sheedah's voice rang out.

She marched across the foyer floor.

"What are you doing?"

"He attacked me," Talcen said.

"No, I didn't, you idiot!"

[LOCKDOWN IN EFFECT]

"Would someone shut the announcement off?" Darrovan screamed.

The sentry's visor turned to him.

"You placed your hands on me and came forward in an aggressive manner. This is quintessential to an impending attack."

"That doesn't justify hitting him," Sheedah countered as she came to a stop by them.

"It does in my book."

"Which book?"

"The military one."

Talcen shifted on his feet, addressing Sheedah.

"What are you doing here? The elevator's off-limits in a lockdown."

"You don't say. I came to see if there was something wrong. I couldn't raise Lias in the dome and figured he might come here to head off anyone trying to flee."

"He's not here."

"I think I could've figured that out for myself."

Sheedah knelt beside Darrovan, a hand rubbing his back.

"Are you okay?"

He blinked a few times and nodded.

"Yeah, I'll be alright."

"He said Lias is dead."

Sheedah didn't respond.

Darrovan glanced at her as he rose.

Her face went slack, the scales rippling in her cheeks. She turned haunted eyes to him. The scarlet brilliance etched her horrified features.

"Is this true?"

A pang of anguish went through him, drowning out the immediate worry of the miasma below.

"I'm so sorry."

He reached for her, but she backed away.

"Did you do this?"

"What? No!"

"I think he snapped," Talcen said. "The dome has a way of getting to people."

Darrovan glanced between the two.

"You're crazy. Why would I hurt Lias, let alone kill him? Look at me! I'm not even strong. I give lectures at a college, not grapple with warriors."

Talcen cocked his head.

"A young man against a feeble, old one. It's pretty easy to figure out who would win."

"But I haven't even had training."

Sheedah interrupted, "How do you know?"

Darrovan shook his head, trying to put it into words, but Talcen answered when he didn't speak up fast enough.

"He says he heard it over the speakers."

Sheedah's accusatory eyes swept over him.

"How?"

"I can't say."

"Where were you?"

"In the vault."

"That's easy enough to determine. We can look at the logs in the dome."

She glanced at the military guard.

"Talcen, place him in cuffs until we sort this out."

"You must be joking!"

The panic from earlier returned.

If you don't come to me, Darrovan, I know someone who will!

[LOCKDOWN IN EFFECT]

"We've got to go before it's too late!"

Sheedah pulled a communicator from her belt and paused.

"Why, again?"

Darrovan ground his teeth.

"I can't say."

"Uh-huh."

She turned away, talking into her device.

"Place your hands behind your back," Talcen instructed.

Darrovan turned. "No." He shoved the sentry away. "This is—"

Another wave of pain hit him, and blackness took him.

Raised voices roused him from oblivion.

When he opened his eyes again, his cheek lay against the cold, familiar black floor of the dome.

Lias's office.

"He's my patient."

"I don't care," Talcen said.

"As lead physician of this facility, I have direct authority over all personnel in a medical situation. This is one of those times, and I'm invoking my authority. He's unconscious and bleeding. Further, he was treated for a bite last night."

"Perhaps he got an infection—and it drove him crazy?"

Brelo scoffed.

"You military loafers are all the same, as keen as a dull scalpel."

Footsteps came closer.

"Darrovan, can you hear me?"

He muttered a groggy reply as she turned him on his side.

He focused on her.

"My head hurts."

She gave a sardonic grin.

"I'm sure that's not all."

[LOCKDOWN IN EFFECT]

"I'm going to give you another shot, some more antibiotics and a pain reliever. You'll be a little groggy, but still functional."

A few moments later, he felt the prick in his arm.

"Honestly, if you wanted to see me again, there are easier ways than getting beat up by Talcen."

She smiled.

"You should've come in after breakfast. It would've been a perfectly valid excuse."

Brelo turned towards people beyond Darrovan's eyesight.

"Are you going to uncuff him or not?"

"No," Talcen said in a flat voice.

"Talcen, do it," Sheedah said, her voice shaky.

"I answer only to Lias."

"He's dead, isn't he?" Sheedah interjected.

"The chain of command is broken. All requests are funneled through the highest-ranking military member. That's me."

"This isn't a military operation," Brelo said, standing. "It's a government operation with expert scientists. Your job is security. Command falls to Sheedah as Head of Operations."

"That's correct—security is my arena," Talcen agreed. "And until we discover how Lias died, I'm securing the prisoner. That has nothing to do with operations."

"I've told you," Brelo said, "it's impossible for him to have killed Lias."

"And the log shows Darrovan was speaking the truth," Sheedah added. "He did get on the elevator from the vault and came straight to the lobby."

"People don't just die on their own," Talcen countered.

Darrovan stirred, the drugs coursing through him. He tried to follow what they were saying, but …

Darrovan.

He shook his head, blocking out the miasma's voice. The contact sparked a seed of worry.

We're all going to die.

[LOCKDOWN IN EFFECT]

"It was Zhidur," he said, rising to his knees, a difficult feat with his hands bound behind him. Now that he could see them, he saw Guinnian had arrived, too.

"Who's Zhidur," Guinnian asked, his hands steepled under his chin.

"We don't have anyone registered by that name," Talcen said. "How do you know this person killed Lias? How did they breach the dome or bypass our security measures?"

Darrovan shook his head.

"You've all had it wrong. It's always been here. We've got to leave."

"We're going—" Talcen began, but Sheedah waved him away.

"What are you talking about?"

Darrovan chewed his lip.

"It has to do with the vault."

"Professor, need I remind you—" Guinnian began.

"We don't have time for formalities!" Darrovan yelled.

"I told you. Unhinged," Talcen intoned.

"What about the vault?" Sheedah inquired, stepping closer.

She knelt in front of him.

"Does it have something to do with my—" she stopped, "Lias?"

He nodded, and she paled.

Hooking her hand under his arm, she helped him stand. On his feet, she guided him to where Lias lay.

"Did whatever's down below do this?"

Darrovan lost control of his insides, and he hurled on the floor.

Lias lay in a heap, his body bent and twisted.

"Talcen, release him," Sheedah implored.

"You must surely realize I can't."

"We don't have time for this," Brelo interjected. "Darrovan, what aren't you telling us?"

"It was the miasma," he breathed, sucking in some of the bile he just expunged.

He spat on the floor a few times, trying to dislodge the residue.

"You can't discuss what happens in the vault," Guinnian protested. "I doubted your intellect when you arrived, but now you've proved the justification in my assumption."

"What's in the vault?" Talcen asked.

"You can't ask that!" Guinnian said.

"A thing of nightmares," Darrovan whispered. "We're all going to die if you don't start listening to me."

"So, we have a security breach?"

The speakers overhead crackled to life.

"Help!" a woman shrieked. "He's out! He's killing everyone—"

The comm cut off.

"Who's that?" Sheedah asked.

Brelo turned white.

"The infirmary! That was Dr. Wimkei's voice."

[LOCKDOWN IN EFFECT]

"Somebody shut that damn thing off!" Darrovan snapped.

"We need to get down there," Sheedah said. "Talcen, release Darrovan. He's clearly not the culprit of Lias's attack or this one."

Talcen shook his head as he stepped forward. Darrovan turned so he could unlock the handcuffs, but the sentry didn't. Instead, he bent down and pulled Lias's black badge from his chest.

"What are you doing?" Sheedah inquired in a high voice.

"You heard the professor."

He stood and waded deeper into the room, stopping in front of a computer console.

"You all need to head to the rendezvous point. It's level seven. The others should be waiting for you there."

He typed in a command.

[LOCKDOWN IN EFFECT. Reminders are set for maximum delay of ten-minute intervals.]

"What do you plan to do?" Guinnian asked, his steepled fingers tapping together.

Talcen turned for the elevator.

"We've got a security breach in the vault. My job's to take care of it."

"If you go down there, it'll kill you," Darrovan warned.

This was crazy. How could Talcen march down there knowing he could die?

"We've got to help the people in the infirmary," Brelo added.

"I am; it's on the way," Talcen said as he got to the elevator.

He pushed the button. The doors parted, and he stepped in.

"Are you coming?"

Chapter 8: It Isn't Standard Issue

The doors parted, and all within the elevator gasped.

A disarrayed infirmary greeted them.

Glass shards covered the floor, a peppering of sharp glitter. The red light flickered in and out. Small fluorescent lights clinging to the underside of cabinets were torn off. A few stray sparks fizzled each time the power fluctuated.

Several scents wafted through the air, something Darrovan couldn't quite describe or pinpoint. He breathed through his mouth; it didn't obscure the strange odors, but it took the brunt of it away.

Despite the seemingly organic scents mixed with the once-sterile environment, there was something unnatural in the air.

The patient's bed in the main chamber was flipped over. A bloodied arm still in its lab coat lay on the floor, ripped away at the shoulder. Dark smears covered the deck, blackened pools streaked by the bodies dragged away.

The panic he'd tried to smother floated back to the surface. His body trembled with adrenaline.

The scales on Darrovan's back quivered.

"We've got to get out of here."

Talcen's faceless visor turned to him.

"You keep saying so but never elaborate."

Darrovan balked.

"What part of 'we're going to die' needs elaboration?"

"Shh," Sheedah hissed.

Darrovan winced, realizing how loud he spoke.

It was stupid and careless. He might as well announce to everyone where they were.

"Come on," Talcen said, leading the way.

He stepped into the foyer. His visor turned, scanning the environment. Brelo followed with timid steps, her head jerking to the sides with each sound.

Sheedah waited a few more moments, then exited as well, standing tall and straight. Darrovan marveled at her bravery. If only he could be so bold.

Darrovan glanced at the remaining occupant in the elevator, Guinnian.

"Aren't you coming?" the professor asked.

A smirk covered the lead researcher's features. "The smart stay alive because the mentally feeble are filled with heroic dreams."

Ire mingled with anxiety and stress, and Darrovan frowned.

"You're an asshole, you know that?"

Finding courage to exit the elevator and follow Sheedah, he advanced.

"Rather be an asshole and alive than a brilliant, dead scientist."

Guinnian tapped his fingers together, the grin widening across his face.

"Yeah, but Talcen's the only one with a gun."

The smirk vanished, and Guinnian hurried after them, thrusting himself into the middle of the group and right behind Talcen.

The sentry's head swiveled halfway behind him as if checking for danger, then moved deeper into the room.

Probably the smartest thing Guinnian's done since I got here.

His eyes roved the remains of the massacre. Among the gore, medical supplies lay strewn as if tossed by an otherworldly gust.

Syringes, broken bottles of pills, and gauze pads cluttered the unseemly scene. Vials of liquid oozed, their fragile encasings adding to the brittle crystalline covering the ground.

"Did you catch that?" Sheedah asked.

The group stopped, straining to listen. Talcen spoke first.

"No, what?"

"I heard something, a voice." In breathier tones, she continued, "It whispered my name."

"I—I didn't hear anything," Brelo stammered, her head darting back and forth.

Oh, God! This can't be happening.

"There it is again," Sheedah said, anxiety riddling her voice.

She peered down the curving hallway to the right.

"I think it's Calistor."

A sinking feeling nestled in the pit of Darrovan's stomach. He shook his head.

"I don't think so."

Sheedah took a few steps forward.

"Calistor? Is that you?"

The lights flared again.

"Calistor?"

"Get back," Darrovan urged, but she continued forward.

He would've snatched her by the arm had he not been handcuffed. He did the next best thing he could think of.

"Talcen, what's wrong with you?" Brelo asked. "Go after her. Get her to come back."

The mirrored visor shifted towards him.

"Stay here."

He plodded after Sheedah.

"Don't leave," Guinnian pleaded.

"Yeah, that's a great idea," Darrovan muttered. "Let's split up. Totally normal in these types of situations."

His eyes darted around the gloomy room.

"Nothing could ever go wrong in a room torn apart with body parts lying everywhere."

His eyes searched for any sign of movement or clues they might've missed.

Brelo, having regained her composure, turned to the lead researcher.

"We'll be fine. Don't worry."

"What?" Darrovan asked. He eyed her. "We have every reason to worry, don't you see the bodies?"

Brelo's brows rose.

"No, I don't, and neither do you. I only see body *parts*, which might be a good thing."

"Really?"

The scales along his neck quivered as his eyes returned to the severed arm.

"Yes, that means those who were in here might've found a way to keep safe. Maybe they locked themselves in a room?"

She padded deeper into the foyer, near the patient bed and cleaved arm.

It would be just my luck that the arm reaches out for her right about now.

"I don't think the person with one arm's locking themselves in a room anytime soon," he said under his breath.

He peered at the hallway on the right. Talcen and Sheedah disappeared beyond the curve.

Damn, what the hell was wrong with them? They were stronger and safer in numbers.

Though the lights down the halls fluctuated, the overhead bulb in the foyer remained relatively constant. Every once in a while, it would dim a touch with the unsteady power.

Standing in the center of the junction of hallways didn't make him feel any safer. He warred with the notion of going into the foyer with the doctor near the amputated limb.

He glanced down both hallways before hurrying to Brelo's side. Self-preservation in numbers won out. Brelo reached for the arm, examining it.

Darrovan's stomach churned, and he was glad he didn't eat a big breakfast.

Yeah, let's pick up the arm—why not?

A sinister thought flitted through his head.

What if Zhidur could animate it? It's so close to her neck, it could reach out and choke her.

The broken glass tinkered, and both Brelo and Darrovan jumped. Guinnian took a few steps closer.

Both shot him a vehement glare.

"What?"

"You scared the shit out of me," Darrovan said.

A smug smirk stretched across Guinnian's face.

"Look at this," Brelo said, turning back to the arm. "This isn't cut or severed but ripped out. Who could do this?"

"Someone who isn't in control of themselves," Darrovan said.

His mind turned back to Calistor and the incident when the catatonic patient bit into his shoulder.

The lights sputtered again, this time staying out for a long three seconds. They sputtered to life.

Darrovan's body tightened with worry, muscles aching. He flexed his fingers, the tips going numb.

[LOCKDOWN IN EFFECT] the loud automated voice said, causing them to jump.

"Damn it!"

Brelo gave a sympathetic glance.

Guinnian spoke, "Don't be so skittish, Professor."

Darrovan's heart hammered, nearly coming up his throat. After the voice, an eerie quiet fell. Guinnian turned his head in the direction Sheedah and Talcen departed.

"What's taking them so long?"

Who's skittish now?

Darrovan glanced in that direction. Apprehension enveloped him. Guinnian was right.

"Better yet, why can't we hear them?"

Brelo stood, her voice small and quiet, "Do you think something happened to them?"

Darrovan shook his head.

"I don't know. Shouldn't we have heard something?"

A shadow deepened in the corner of his eye. A flicker of movement and the absence of sound constricted him with fear. He jerked his head to Guinnian.

"Behind you!"

A spray of hot blood coated Darrovan's face. A clawed fist burst through Guinnian's chest. He gasped, his large dark eyes wide.

"But—"

The clawed hand jerked free. Guinnian crumbled to the floor. Calistor stood behind him, dark fluid covering his clothes.

"Shit!"

"Help!" Brelo screamed.

Calistor's mouth opened, revealing sharp teeth.

Darrovan's throat closed, remembering how they ripped into him. His wound ached in remembrance.

Calistor unfurled his arms, his claws glistening.

He launched himself at Darrovan.

They tumbled to the floor. His wounded shoulder popped with a rush of heat. Calistor straddled his chest. He raised a clawed hand.

"Shit, shit, shit!"

"Get off him!" Brelo yelled.

She snatched up the arm and bashed Calistor in the head.

Claws cut through the air as he lashed out. Three ribbons of furrowed flesh blossomed on her face.

Brelo fell back, screaming.

Calistor turned back to Darrovan. His jaw opened, lips peeling back, revealing glistening teeth.

A loud explosion rang out. Light flashed in the dim room. Another spray of blood coated Darrovan's face, warm and copious. Some fell into his mouth, rolled about his tongue as he tried to spit.

He shook his head, eyes fluttering open.

Calistor's head was split in two, a deep gash down the middle. His body flailed, arms twitching.

He crumbled, coming to rest atop Darrovan.

Through the gruesome, fleshy cavity of bone, blood, and brain matter, Darrovan spied Talcen standing behind with his blaster still smoking.

"Oh, my God! Calistor!" Sheedah shrieked.

She rushed forward, pulling her cousin off Darrovan. She wept, holding his body.

Darrovan squirmed on the floor, trying to find his feet. His bound hands made that difficult, as did the blood-slickened floor.

"Help me, damn you!" he shouted at Talcen.

The sentry came over and pulled him up by one arm. Pain shot through Darrovan's shoulder, and he winced.

"What?" Talcen asked.

"My shoulder and arm. I think it's dislocated or broken."

Now that the adrenaline started to wear off, it ached all the more. Darrovan focused on Sheedah, who still cradled Calistor's remains.

He eyed Talcen.

"What kept you?"

"We were at the end of the hallway. I'd say we made excellent time, don't you?"

A weak cough filled the silence. Everyone turned to Guinnian, who spat up blood, choking.

"Oh, Guinnian," Brelo said in a pain-laced voice. She crawled over the broken glass, and rolled him to his side. Blood pooled underneath her hands as she did.

Darrovan winced with sympathetic pain. If she didn't feel it now, she would later.

"Is—Is—it bad?" he gasped.

Darrovan hurried over, getting a good look at Brelo's face. The claw marks were superficial, but she still bled.

She'd have scars forever.

One track missed her right eye by centimeters. His eyes roamed to Guinnian. The entire shirt was coated in blood.

Brelo pressed a hand to the wound. "You'll be fine."

Darrovan wasn't a doctor, but he could tell she was lying. In the final moments, Guinnian would have hope.

"Who keeps calling my name?" Sheedah croaked.

Darrovan's head snapped to her. Tears streaked her face.

"I—I—hear—it, too." Guinnian coughed.

"What're you all talking about?" Talcen asked. "I don't detect anything."

"It's the miasma, the Dark Portal," Darrovan answered. "Zhidur. Down in the vault."

"You—you idiot," Guinnian rasped.

Darrovan's head turned to the lead researcher.

"Oh, hmm, rude?"

And then, he lay still.

"Fuck!" Brelo cried, pulling blood-soaked hands away.

She used the back of her hand against the bridge of her nose.

"What the hell's going on? This is the second time Calistor's hurt or killed someone. How's that possible? I put him in a straight jacket myself. Can anyone tell me?"

Talcen spoke up, ignoring her.

"Let's see if I understand this correctly. Sheedah and Guinnian have a voice talking in their head? What about you, Professor? Are you crazy, too?"

Horror lanced him. What would Talcen say if he said yes? Then, anger flared in him.

"Two people are dead, asshole. Three if you count Lias. Don't you have a conscience?"

Talcen cocked his head.

"It isn't standard-issued."

Darrovan stepped closer to him, coming face to face.

"I'd fucking hit you right now if I wasn't handcuffed. This isn't the time for jokes."

"Who said I was joking? Besides, you *are* handcuffed, and there's nothing you can do about it."

Talcen pressed two fingers in the bite wound on Darrovan's dislocated left shoulder. The professor winced in pain, and he staggered back from the guard.

"Now, about the voice and this thing in the vault."

Darrovan groaned.

"We've got to leave. Don't you understand? It's an alien! There's an alien inside this base, and it's talking to them in their head."

"What?" Sheedah asked from behind, her voice shaking. "What're you talking about? I thought they were working on some kind of portal device."

"Lias called it the Dark Portal, that's where you might've heard the term portal."

Darrovan sighed.

"If that's all it was, a way to travel, then why the hell would he want me here?"

He shook his head.

"I'm here to talk to an extraterrestrial. Find out what it wants."

"What does it want?" Talcen asked.

"I think it's getting what it wants. Us. Dead."

Talcen turned and headed for the elevator.

"Head for the rendezvous point."

The doors parted, and he entered.

"Where are you going?"

Talcen turned, swiped Lias's black badge, and pushed a button.
"To kill an alien."
The doors closed.

Chapter 9: The Infirmary

"Why would he be sending us to level seven?"

The elevator whirled behind Brelo.

"That's the brig."

A sniffle rose from Sheedah.

"It's standard procedure."

She turned her back and knelt beside Calistor.

"Other than the vault, it's the most secure place in the facility. He's right; the others will muster there."

An echo of the pain in his left shoulder reminded Darrovan of Calistor's bite. He eyed the corpse. His legs trembled with the memory of almost being bitten again. The handcuffs didn't help, either.

Darrovan.

A terrible notion hit Darrovan.

Can the miasma animate a body?

"Is that it?" Sheedah asked in breathless tones.

Her voice trembled. She glanced up at the ceiling.

"Is that the alien?"

Darrovan turned to her, and he could see the fear radiating from her.

"You heard Zhidur call me?"

She shook her head.

"No, it called my name."

"Mine, too," Brelo added.

"We need to go. This place isn't safe," Darrovan persisted. "We should head to level seven as fast as possible, and then make a break for the surface."

"I agree," Brelo said. "If it can talk to us, control Calistor, we aren't safe."

She waded deeper into the central foyer, rummaging through drawers.

"What are you doing?" Darrovan asked.

"I'm looking for a surgical torch. The laser should be powerful enough to cut through your cuffs, but it'll take a bit."

Appreciation and surprise rippled through him.

"Yes, please. That'd be great."

Brelo began opening drawers, shoving tools, and supplies aside while she searched.

A gush of breath escaped Sheedah—one of weariness and heartache. Darrovan sympathized. He peered down at Calistor. It wasn't the poor chap's fault; he became a puppet of Zhidur, and to Darrovan's surprise, he didn't hold any animosity towards Lias's nephew.

His eyes tracked to Sheedah, who was on the verge of tears. In one day, a span of minutes, really, she lost her father and her cousin.

"Ah," Brelo said, finding the surgical torch.

Darrovan looked up, and she motioned him closer.

"Turn around, hop up on the bed, and hold still."

He did.

The laser fired up with a slight hum. As the plasma cut through the metal, a hiss accompanied by an acrid scent rose up.

Sheedah wiped her face and stood, turning to Darrovan.

"How's it talking to us?"

Darrovan started to shake his head but stopped, remembering he shouldn't move.

"I don't know. Zhidur called to me while I slept."

Sheedah's eyes went wide, and she padded closer, leaving her cousin's body behind.

"What do you mean?"

"One link down," Brelo announced.

The hiss started again, and the foul scent grew stronger.

"It called to me, wanted me to come to the vault, but I didn't."

Sheedah's eyes darted back to the elevator.

"Do you think Talcen's influenced, that the alien called him? Is he obeying its edicts now?"

The thought never crossed Darrovan's mind. A new level of dread hardened in the pit of his stomach.

That's a perfect capper. The only one with a gun might be duped into being a pawn. But if he isn't, he won't survive the encounter with Zhidur.

"Do you think he lied about not hearing the voice?" Brelo asked. "I mean, he was rather condescending about it."

The cuffs gave way, and Darrovan's hands released with a jerk. The sudden movement shot agony through his lacerated shoulder, and he winced.

"Still in pain? I can give you another shot."

"Please?" he agreed with a nod.

He gazed at Sheedah.

"I don't know. He could be lying, but he's acting the same as he always has, at least from what I can tell. You have more history with him than I do. You tell me."

Sheedah shook her head.

"Not much. I've never seen him in a social setting. Brelo?"

Darrovan caught the shake of her head as she prepared another shot. Sheedah's eyes narrowed and scrutinized him.

"Do you think the alien tried to control you?"

Darrovan shrugged, wincing again.

"It's possible."

"How did you fight the impulse?"

The needle pierced his scaly flesh, a pinpoint of fire in his shoulder. Both Sheedah and the professor's attention went to the injection. Brelo depressed the syringe in a steady movement, then withdrew the needle. She stepped over to the counter in the back of the foyer.

"The pain relievers?" he offered, feeling foolish for offering the suggestion.

[LOCKDOWN IN EFFECT]

Sheedah's brow twitched upward in thought.

"You might be on to something."

A clang of metal on the floor made them jump. Darrovan lurched to his feet in an instant.

His eyes snapped to Brelo, down to the metal tray on the ground, and back up.

The doctor turned slowly, a scalpel in her hand. Her arm trembled.

Darrovan glanced at her eyes, seeing her pupils like pinpricks.

"Oh, God," he said. "He's got her, too."

"What?" Sheedah asked, her voice high with hysteria.

"She's under the alien's control."

Darrovan backed away, pulling Sheedah with his healthy arm.

"He keeps calling me," Brelo said in a shaky voice.

Tears streamed down her face. She took a staggering step forward.

"Help me!"

Another step.

"Oh, shit," Darrovan said, glancing around the room for a weapon.

Something caught his heels, and he tripped. He landed hard on his backside. A jolt of pain shot through his spine. Calistor's legs caused the stumble, and for once, Darrovan was glad he stayed dead.

"What do we do?" Sheedah implored in panic.

Brelo was about to kill them with Sheedah useless with delirium. They were weaponless, and Talcen, their one protector, was gone.

"What do we do?" Sheedah repeated.

"We've got to detain her, give her an injection."

Darrovan rose to his feet.

"Will it work?"

"Your guess is as good as mine!" he shouted.

It was only a theory. He wasn't cut out for this. He had no military experience, no fighting skills, and the wound made him less than useful.

Brelo sobbed as she took another step forward.

"He wants you, Darrovan."

Her arm trembled.

"I'm trying to fight the impulse."

Darrovan moved to the left, around the patient bed, keeping the furniture between him and the doctor.

Sheedah, seeing him, shifted in the opposite direction, hugging the wall to the right.

Brelo turned to him and continued forward. Her steps came faster but in jerking movements.

"Fight it, Brelo. Fight Zhidur!"

Tears streamed her face.

"I can't."

Another two quick steps. She cleared the bed. Darrovan backed against the left wall. Brelo staggered forward again, cutting off his escape through the entrance. Her arms and legs twitched like a marionette controlled by a drunken puppeteer.

Another stride.

"I'm sorry," she cried.

"You're better than this," Darrovan yelled. "Fight, damn you!"

Another movement forward, she stood less than six feet away now.

Darrovan shifted to the left again, towards the back of the room. He ran into a plastic and metal chair, the seat hitting him in the knees. He snatched it up to keep her away.

Another footstep.

"I'm so sorry, Darrovan. Please forgive me."

Another hitch forward, the legs of the chair pressed against her chest.

She raised the scalpel, her arm shook the whole way.

"No," Darrovan screamed. "No!"

Brelo spasmed. Her arm twitched, plunging down. It stopped, shaking in midair.

Pain lanced Brelo's face.

Behind her, Sheedah stood, a needle buried deep in the doctor's neck, the other hand holding the doctor's wrist.

Brelo's fingers released the scalpel, and it clattered to the floor. Sheedah withdrew the needle, and Brelo gasped in relief.

She sank to her knees and sobbed, her body convulsing.

"I'm so sorry, Darrovan."

The professor balked at Sheedah.

She gave a nod and walked to the back of the room, preparing another injection. He knelt in front of his would-be attacker. He cupped her chin, lifting her face.

"It's okay," he soothed. "You did well. You fought him off long enough for us to help you."

She cried all the harder.

He shuffled closer, running his good hand up and down her back. He didn't know what to say. Having never married or dated, females were as alien as Zhidur.

In a sudden movement, Brelo clung to him, hugging and sobbing.

He peered back at Sheedah.

A bemused look covered her face, then she cringed as she stuck the needle in her arm. A sigh of relief washed through Darrovan. They were all safe from control for the time being, but others resided in the dome.

"How many people are here?" he asked Sheedah.

She rubbed her arm. "Maybe thirty of us total."

"Including Lias and the others?"

Her eyes turned to Calistor's corpse.

"Twenty-seven," she amended.

Darrovan pulled back from Brelo.

"Doctor? Other people need your help."

Her whimpers receded to small gasps.

"Did you hear Sheedah? Twenty-seven others need our help and injections. If we don't, that's twenty-seven more who might try to kill us. I need you to gather enough supplies to take with us to the brig. Can you do that?"

She nodded, hugged him again, and climbed to her feet. She ambled back to the medicine cabinets, her steps confident.

He watched her go and climbed to his feet.

It's incredible what purpose can do for people. I wonder what purpose the military gives to drones like Talcen.

The moment he thought it, he felt terrible.

Talcen left, facing off with an alien who intended to kill them all. Despite numerous warnings, Talcen went knowingly to his death.

If anything, he deserved Darrovan's respect.

Sheedah came over and handed him a sling.

"For your arm."

"Thank you."

He unfolded the cloth, took a moment to figure out how to put it on, and slipped his arm through. As he put the strap across his neck, an unsettling thought entered his mind.

"Twenty-seven personnel. That's not very many working here. What about the families? How many of those are children?"

Sheedah's dark, expressive eyes blinked at him.

"What families?"

"The kids that are here. I thought you said this place was like a resort for families who come here with their parents."

She shook her head, confusion etching her face.

"No, I never said that. I said we have an entertainment-resort level, but I never mentioned children."

"But ..." Darrovan frowned, remembering Kavisha and her little clue about hatchlings. "...What about Kavisha and her kids?"

"Who?"

"Kavisha! The scientist. What about her and her hatchlings?"

"Hatchlings?"

Worry etched Sheedah's face.

"That's an odd—"

"I realize that," he said, cutting her off. "But that's what she said. She called her children hatchlings. I assumed she came from a religious —"

Darrovan.

The professor's eyes widened.

"Trust me," Sheedah said, "we don't have anyone here by that name. And there certainly aren't children here."

His knees grew weak.

"Oh, God."

"What?"

His hand reached out to the chair to steady himself.

"It was the alien. Zhidur."

"What are you talking about?"

82

Darrovan.

His head snapped up.

"Don't you get it?"

He laughed something that wasn't his own. Did the mirth come from Zhidur?

"You're starting to worry me."

"The miasma."

He took a few deep breaths.

"I don't understand."

"From the moment I got here," he explained, tapping his head, "it's been fiddling with me. Don't you get it? I met a woman named Kavisha in the vault below. We talked, and she said some things I thought were off, but I ignored them because I was paranoid. Now, I realize the alien made me see her and talked to me, probing my mind before I entered the room."

Brelo joined them, a hefty medical bag slung over her shoulder.

"That's disconcerting, if true."

He nodded.

"Yeah, and now its got me second-guessing everything."

His eyes flickered to Calistor's lifeless form.

"Lias said the alien attacked Calistor. How long ago did that happen before I arrived? A few weeks, right?"

Sheedah blinked a few times. With a slow shake of her head, she answered.

"Hours. The attack happened that morning, and sometime during the night, you arrived."

Darrovan paled. The blood drained from his face.

"You can't be serious?"

Sheedah nodded.

Darrovan tightened his grip on the chair, letting the claws dig in deep. He slammed it down, anger bursting out.

"Your father let me go into that fucking room hours after the attack on your cousin?"

"Cousin?" Brelo echoed.

Her eyes darted between the two.

"Lias ... was your father?"

Sheedah nodded, wincing in Brelo's direction. "Yes, that's why he had Calistor's medical records sealed, so you wouldn't make the connection."

Brelo let the bag fall to the floor.

83

"That bastard! He said we couldn't have family here. I've gone through a divorce because of him."

Sheedah held up her hands, shaking her head.

"I'm sorry. It wasn't my call."

"What exactly do you do here?" Darrovan asked, pushing away from the chair. "What function do you serve?"

Sheedah's face steeled, and she straightened.

"I serve as second in command. I ensure the safety of all personnel, their files, and property within the dome. In the off chance we're invaded by the government or some outside force, it's my job to destroy everything within to save the identity of all who worked here."

"Plausible deniability," Brelo said, her voice distant. "Son of a bitch."

"Yes."

"And how would you keep everyone's identity a secret if we're being attacked? That's a lot of hardware to wipe."

She shrugged.

"There are many methods, each more drastic than the last. If there's no hope to repel the forces, we set the self-destruct, and let the dome implode."

Chapter 10: Duty

Sheedah's words thundered in his ears.

The red glare overhead, which still winked in and out, didn't improve his mood.

"There's a self-destruct?" Darrovan asked.

The lights flickered for a moment.

Sheedah started to nod but paused to glance at the lights overhead.

"Yes."

Brelo snatched her by the arm.

"And just when were you going to tell us this?"

"Never."

"Sounds about right," Darrovan muttered.

He rolled his eyes.

Indignation flashed across Sheedah's face, but she cringed and clutched her head.

Darrovan.

The professor eyed the reactions of the others. The portal still spoke to them.

"I take it Talcen wasn't successful."

Deh la noss Enu Brek Zhiem-la-dur! Answer me, Darrovan. I command it!

"What the fuck do you want?" Darrovan hollered.

Beish gul, Darrovan.

He shook his head as if the miasma could see him.

"Yeah, I don't think so."

"If Talcen's dead," Sheedah began, "he left with the only weapon. It's still down there."

"You can understand him?" Brelo asked. "All I hear's gibberish."

He shook his head. "Not really. More like he can understand us. Every once in a while, something clear will come through."

"What's he saying?" Brelo asked.

"I don't—something and his name."

"How do you know it's a him?" Sheedah inquired.

Darrovan gave Sheedah a blank expression.

"I don't. It's figurative. Really? We're going to discuss the alien's sex right now? There are far more important things to quibble over."

Sheedah shrank back, her face full of shame.

The elevator doors parted, and the group spun around. Without looking, Darrovan snatched up the chair, holding it as a shield and weapon.

Talcen's visor stared back at them.

"What are you still doing here? I told you to rendezvous on level seven. Why didn't you go?"

"You're back," Sheedah said, breathing a sigh of relief.

She pointed and eyed Darrovan.

"And he's still got the blaster."

"Obviously," Talcen quipped. "Why didn't you go to level seven like I told you?"

Sheedah took a step forward to speak, but Darrovan cut in.

"How'd you know we didn't go?"

The sentry's visor turned in his direction.

"There's only one elevator, Professor. It was still in the vault level when I boarded it. I'm no genius like Guinnian, but it wasn't hard to figure out."

He paused, and the helmeted figure tilted his head.

"Who removed your cuffs, Professor?"

Brelo stepped forward.

"I did, to treat my patient."

Talcen's visor dipped.

"What's with the bag?"

The group glanced back, and Brelo picked it off the floor.

"I've got supplies for the others. The alien can take control of us, but we found a way around the problem. Everyone needs injections of pain reliever, even you."

Talcen shook his head.

"That's not necessary."

Brelo was about to protest when the sentry spoke again.

"How did you deduce that it works?"

Brelo stammered for a moment.

"The chemical properties inhibit some brain functions by deadening or suppressing certain—"

"No," Talcen interrupted. "How did you figure out it'll work?"

In a rush, Darrovan relayed the tale of what happened in the guard's absence.

"Interesting," he said, more to himself.

"Look, man," Darrovan said, "we need to move. Even if we have a temporary solution, we should use that as our advantage and escape."

"Why didn't you kill the alien?" Sheedah asked.

Now that she voiced it aloud, and Zhidur still spoke to them, Talcen either didn't kill him or was ineffectual. Or worse...

A frisson of tension rose within the trio as they stared at the armed sentry. The same thought that prickled in Darrovan's mind probably entered the others. Talcen could be under Zhidur's control.

"There wasn't an alien," Talcen said after a moment. "I didn't see anything."

Darrovan frowned.

"What do you mean? It was in the vault when I left."

Talcen gave a small shrug.

"Well, it's not there now."

He motioned with his head.

"Come on, the others are waiting on level seven."

Darrovan eyed the women.

What should they do? The ladies gave him long, meaningful looks. Either they were wrong, and Talcen wasn't under control, or they'd go to their deaths if they followed him. Worse, if they refused, and Talcen remained under the alien's sway, he'd gun them down where they stood.

The options warred within Darrovan for a brief moment. The elevator seemed the safest bet. The Dark Portal still called to him, beckoned him to come, and that meant Talcen wouldn't shoot them.

The alien had plans for him.

The lights flickered again, relieving the shadows for a brief moment before plunging the room into darkness.

Zhidur's voice boomed in his head.

Deh la noss Enu Brek Zhiem-la-dur! You will obey or perish.

The doctor and Sheedah covered their ears, cringing as the voice boomed in their head, too.

"I don't understand what the fuck you're saying!" Darrovan roared.

Talcen drew his blaster and pointed.

"What?"

"Don't you hear it?" Brelo asked, her voice full of pain.

"No."

Darrovan took a moment to eye the sentry.

The blaster was out and pointed, but not at them. He swept the room, searching for an enemy. Relief shot through him. They could trust their military member.

At least there's some good news in all this.

Brelo knelt, pulling open the bag. Fumbling for a syringe, she upended the bottle and drew the liquid.

"It's louder, stronger," Sheedah said in a shaky breath.

Her frantic eyes darted around, searching as if the miasma was in the room with them.

"No," Darrovan said.

Ice poured down his spine.

Everything fell into place.

The louder voice, Talcen not seeing the alien in the vault.

"He's closer."

As the words left his mouth, a hiss echoed in the room.

The group gawked at each other for a moment before hurrying out of the foyer. They turned left, down the right hallway. Amid the strobing red light, a billowing black cloud poured from the vents overhead.

"Oh, shit!" Darrovan yelled, pointing.

Before he could say anything else, blaster fire erupted from behind them.

"MOVE!" Talcen shouted, stepping in front of them, clearing the way for the others to retreat.

Darrovan took a step towards the elevator.

Brelo!

She returned to the bag on the floor and fumbled with a syringe and vial. He jerked her to her feet, the syringe in hand, but the bag left forgotten. "Let's go!"

"Wait! The meds."

"There's no time."

He rushed her forward to the elevator.

"I take it this is the alien," Talcen said as he snapped off a few more shots.

At the door, Darrovan spun around and surveyed the room.

Sheedah hadn't moved. She stood rooted on the spot, no doubt in shock from horror. A crackle of energy poured into the room like bottled lightning.

"Sheedah!" Darrovan yelled.

Another handful of shots rang out with no effect. Each bolt ripped through the gaseous cloud. It rippled where the laser went through. The wall behind smoked with holes.

[LOCKDOWN IN EFFECT]

Darrovan regarded the miasma. About half its mass had escaped the vent. He debated on going back for Sheedah.

A dark tendril reached out, snatching her up by the neck. Her feet kicked as she left the ground. Gurgling sounds escaped from her.

Deh la noss Enu Brek Zhiem-la-dur! All shall perish for your treachery, Darrovan!

Talcen took a step out of the elevator.

He fumbled with the control on the weapon, pointed again, and pulled the trigger. The bolt was brighter, wider, hotter.

The sound, deafening.

The miasma shrieked in agony, a sound like metal grinding against metal. Talcen shot again, no doubt trying to free Sheedah from the alien's grip. The miasma recoiled, seemingly losing mass.

The sentry regarded Darrovan. He thrust two key cards in his hand.

"What?"

"One's mine, the other's Lias's," he said.

He turned around and shot twice more.

Sheedah still hovered in the air, her body still twitching, fighting for life and breath.

Talcen glanced back.

"Lias's will light up the fourteenth floor. That's where the self destruct is. It'll level this place."

So many questions flooded through Darrovan.

"You knew?"

"It was a military base before a research facility."

A sickening crunch drew their attention. Sheedah's head lolled to the side at an odd angle. Her limbs began twisting, bent in ways not intended.

Talcen shot another four blasts. Again, the agony thundered in Darrovan's head.

"Let's leave!" Brelo cried.

"Not without Talcen," Darrovan snapped. "Let's go!" he called to the guard.

"I won't abandon my duty," the other said.

By now, the miasma was almost all the way into the room, flooding in from the ceiling.

"I've got to stop the alien. It's my job."

"Fuck the job!" Brelo screamed. "Get in! Close the door!"

But Darrovan knew the sentry wouldn't. The military ingrained duty into him, hardwired from day one. He'd give his life to protect them.

"What's the other key card?"

"Mine," Talcen said. His blaster ripped through the air again, another pair of shots. The miasma recoiled.

Deh la noss Enu Brek Zhiem-la-dur! You dare strike me? You'll pay for your insolence!

Darrovan winced at the voice thundering in his head.

"What's it do?"

Talcen shot again. "The main elevator. Take everyone from level seven, set the self-destruct, and evacuate! You'll have five minutes. Go!"

He turned and fired again, but this time, he didn't stop. He walked toward the dark cloud and kept firing.

A shadowy tendril reached out and snatched him up.

Darrovan slapped the overseer's badge against the reader.

"Welcome, Lias."

The fourteenth floor lit up as Talcen promised. He mashed the seventh floor. The others were waiting for them.

Deh la!

Darrovan clutched his head as the words reverberated through his skull.

I am!

Another handful of shots rang out.

Darrovan gaped as the doors began to shut.

The tendril slammed Talcen against the wall before lurching him in the opposite direction, heaving him through the glass.

Deh la noss Enu!

I am the Dark!

The miasma shook Talcen like a rag doll.

"Oh, my God, he's got to be dead," Brelo whimpered.

Still, Talcen struggled, firing off another handful of shots.

How's he even alive?

Another tendril snaked out, grabbing the sentry's feet. In a mighty heave, Talcen ripped in two.

A potent rage swept over Darrovan, knocking him on his backside.

The last thing Darrovan saw were the wires jutting out of Talcen's body.

Deh la noss Enu Brek Zhiem-la-dur!

I am the Dark Lord Xilor!

The miasma lurched for them.

The elevator doors closed.

Chapter 11: I Found You

"Oh shit, oh fuck, oh shit," Brelo said over and over.

The elevator sank lower into the facility.

She rocked back and forth where she sat.

It's shock.

Darrovan had seen such effects before, but not quite like this.

His legs trembled. Fatigue rolled over his body. Not for the first time that day, he was grateful for the small breakfast. He would've lost control of his stomach a long time ago.

"Hey," he said, hoping to help her out of her state.

He held out a hand, but she didn't seem to notice.

"We're going to fucking die," she whispered. "We're going to fucking die. Oh shit, oh fuck, we're all going to die."

With his right hand, he smacked her in the face, not hard, but enough to grab her attention.

She blinked a few times, glancing up.

He held out the hand.

"We're not dead yet. Keep your shit together—others are counting on us."

He waved the hand in front of her face, and she grabbed hold. With a heave, he helped her to her feet.

"Besides, there's hope. The alien can be hurt."

"Hurt?"

He nodded.

"Talcen cranked his blaster's power setting up, and it hurt Zhidur."

They fell silent for a moment, and then in a shaky breath, Brelo spoke, "But Talcen's blaster was with him when he died."

Damn.

Her breath came in ragged pants.

"Hey?" he spoke again, trying to distract her. "We're not dead, okay? We've still got to get out of here."

She nodded, her lips drawn tight into a thin, white line. She swayed.

He held her close with one arm. The elevator stopped, and the doors parted.

Red light flooded in.

In the distance, white lights flickered overhead. Darrovan, with Brelo clinging to him, took a step out and froze. His throat tightened.

"I've got a bad feeling about this."

Half a second later, Brelo registered what he said, and what they saw. The sharp inhale resounded in the quiet.

"Oh shit, oh shit," she started again.

Corpses picked clean of flesh and muscle spread out before them. White bone littered the floor. Not a shred of blood or entrails could be found. How many stretched before them? A dozen? Two dozen?

"My God," Darrovan uttered. The long shadows of light and bone stretched out like twisted branches of a naked tree.

[LOCKDOWN IN EFFECT] the automated voice called through the speakers.

Darrovan.

He closed his eyes, willing the voice away.

You cannot hide forever.

A fleeting moment shot through Darrovan. He glanced at Brelo. She still clutched the syringe. He wrestled it away, stuck it in his wounded arm, and depressed half of the medicine. He pulled the needle out, twisted it to face Brelo.

She jerked.

"No, you need a clean needle."

He threw up his hands.

"Do we have one of those lying around?"

I'm coming for you, Darrovan.

He jabbed the needle in her arm and emptied the syringe before she protested again.

"That's too much."

With the good arm, he pulled her back the way they came.

"What's the worst that could happen?"

He held Lias's badge up to the reader.

"Welcome, Lias."

On the slick surface beneath the thirteenth floor, the number fourteen lit up. Without giving it much thought, he pressed the metal.

"Level fourteen," the voice overhead said. "Failsafe floor."

The hatch slid closed on the graveyard of bones and descended once more.

He shook his head.

All those people died because an alien escaped. They were all fools, Lias on down. Himself included. How did they fool themselves into containing an alien, and a gaseous one at that? How did everyone miss the ventilation in the room?

"Loss of motor skills," Brelo began, breaking into his thoughts.

"What?"

"You asked what's the worse that could happen? We could lose motor skills."

More great news.

Did he just doom them?

"Yeah, that doesn't sound so bad," he lied, hoping to keep her preoccupied. "What else?"

You're right, Darrovan.

He frowned as the Dark Portal spoke to him.

There are others, countless worlds. Yours is but one.

"Then, why have you come?" he asked. He chastened himself for the moment of curiosity. Brelo's head snapped up in his direction, an expression of bewilderment stretched across her face.

A ripple of glee lanced through Darrovan, and he knew it was the alien's.

I found you.

"Oh shit."

"What?"

Metal clanged overhead.

Both gazed up.

Judging by the sound, it was too far away to be right on top of them.

"He found us."

Brelo exhaled from her mouth. She reached out for his hand. He glanced down, seeing hers in his. He looked back up, searching her face.

"We're not going to make it out of here, are we?" she asked.

He swallowed.

"I intend to."

A brief pause.

"What will you do if we live?"

The car stopped, and the doors parted. The sudden, bright light made him squint.

He held up a hand to shield his eyes. Directly ahead, no more than half a dozen paces sat a large console.

Beyond that, enclosed in glass, the reactor core crackled with energy. Blue-white energy arced out from the walls, drawn to the center of the room. Though metallic, it resembled a sphere cut in half with the two rounded ends facing each other.

The arcing bolts hit the center where the two half-spheres connected, and the energy raced up the surface in thin, faint lines.

"Stay here," he said.

"Are you kidding? We're not splitting up."

Instead of arguing, he nodded acquiescence.

"Alright."

With laden feet, he stepped out. Brelo followed.

Where are you, Darrovan?

The professor let out a deep breath of relief.

"He can't find us," Brelo said.

"Yeah, I know."

You cannot hide forever.

Darrovan stopped, his eyes on the console. Numerous buttons filled the panel.

How in the hell am I going to figure this out?

Figure what out? Where are you, Darrovan?

A finger of worry propelled him forward. He took the chair.

"Where do I start?" he said, trying to glance at all the buttons at once.

They blinked up at him. He eyed the screens, trying to discern the panel.

"There!" Brelo pointed. "Try the badge reader."

Stupid!

I AM ALL KNOWING!

Darrovan winced at the hate pouring through his mind.

I have bested death.

The professor placed the badge on the reader.

"Welcome, Lias," a male, computerized voice said.

It spoke painfully slow, each word or two felt like it searched its memory banks for the correct word.

"Would you—like to—A:—shutdown the—reactor or—B:—restart the—reactor?"

"Oh, my God, this is going to take forever!" Brelo said, exasperated.

He groaned at how slow the computer spoke.

"Where's the damn self-destruct option?" he blurted.

"Would you—like to—initiate—self-destruct?"

"Yes, where's that option?"

"Standby—one—moment."

The console flickered, the lights dancing in random tangent.

"Please—place the—badge—against the—reader to—initiate—self-destruct."

He did.

"Thank—you."

The lights flickered again.

Darrovan, where are you hiding?

"Can you hurry up?" Brelo asked.

He held up his hands, and the bafflement he felt went to his face.

"Does it look like I'm going slowly on purpose? This thing's archaic."

They waited in silence for a few moments.

When I find you, you'll suffer worse than the metal one.

The memory of Talcen getting ripped in half filled him with dread. How did no one suspect that Talcen was a robot this entire time? But the facts had been staring him in the face all along. Sheedah even said as much.

Darrovan glanced back and noted Talcen's visor watching him. "Don't you worry about insulting the . . ."

"Sentry? Military member?" She shook her head. "No. Talcen isn't a people person. Never mingles. People have been trying to get him to open up for years, but he never does. I don't ever recall seeing him without that helmet on." She sighed. "He's always on duty."

Darrovan's eyes went to the console, a sour twist of his lips coming to his face.

It'd been too long. What kept the console from telling them when the program initiated?

"When's the self-destruct going to start?" he prompted the computer.

"The—self-destruct has—already started."

"Shit!" he jumped up from the chair, and they raced back to the elevator.

The console was still talking.

"You have—three minutes—and—twenty-two—seconds."

Once inside, he moved to swipe the reader, then realized he left Lias's on the console. "Damn it!"

He took a step to run.

"No!" Brelo shouted. "You don't need it! You have yours."

He had forgotten about his badge. He jerked it towards the reader.

"Welcome, Professor."

The gate closed on their own.

"You are in a restricted section."

Darrovan threw his hands up.

"That's just perfect!"

"You will be deposited on the lobby floor. A sentry will be there to take you into custody."

They ascended.

"The lobby?" Brelo asked.

"Yes!" he said, smiling for the first time in he didn't know how long. He raised his arm in the air. "Yes, perfect! That's where we want to go."

Where do you want to go, Darrovan?

The voice boomed in his head, and that meant the miasma was nearby. The lift shuddered, hit by something beneath. Metal groaned in the back corner.

His thoughts turned back to the silent countdown. How much time remained? Were they going to make it out before the explosion?

He and Brelo crowded closer to the hatch, their eyes on the floor. Her arm snaked up, clutching his. The floor rippled, warped, and bent down. A hole formed. Darkness lay beyond.

There's no escape.

"Fuck this shit!" Brelo exclaimed. Another hit rocked the cart. Darrovan's knees bent, absorbing the impact.

He almost fell.

The hole widened. A dark tendril shot through, flailing wildly. Brelo pressed against him, and he tried to back into the door.

The elevator jarred to a halt. The doors parted, and they spilled out.

Brelo made her feet first. She darted back into the lift.

"No!" Darrovan called after her.

A smile crossed her face as she jumped back out. She pulled him up.

"I hit the close door button."

They started running.

The gate closed on the lift, and the clanging of metal followed them. Racing down the hall, they hurried to the lobby. The doors parted as they neared. Dumping out into the main floor, the water fountain gushed, glowing red.

DARROVAN!

They turned left and sprinted. How much time was left now?

Talcen's podium seemed so far away.

His lungs burned.

Running with an arm in a sling proved more difficult than he thought. Metal screeched behind them with a loud thud, and he knew the alien had escaped. The sound of glass breaking and metal being torn from their hinges raced forward, marking the progression of the miasma.

They made it to the main elevator. It seemed like only yesterday, and yet a lifetime ago, that he was here. Darrovan pressed the badge to the reader. The monitor above the doorway read twenty-five and started counting down.

"You've got to be kidding me."

"What?" Brelo followed his gaze. "Oh."

The entryway behind them blew open. The dark cloud spilled out. It rushed forward, towards the fountain and stopped.

Darrovan reached for Brelo, pulling her with him as he ducked down behind Talcen's podium. The miasma circled the fountain, either mesmerized or judging for weaknesses.

Has it never seen a water fountain before?

Maybe they didn't have them where he was from.

Darrovan glanced at the monitor above.

Eighteen.

Once the lift arrived, the doors would open, drawing the alien's attention.

Where are you, Darrovan?

They'd only have one shot, and not long. Who knew how fast the miasma could move?

I came seeking answers, the alien said in his head. *Calistor gave me most of them, but you—you were something more.*

Darrovan glanced back up.

Twelve.

He tried not to think, to let his thoughts wander. Anything might tip off their location.

Calistor's mind was full of incorrect facts and military secrets. The devastation your people can cause cannot be overlooked. You pose a threat. Your mind was filled with delicious paranoia laced with kernels of truth.

The dark cloud circled the fountain, edging closer to the spewing water. Darrovan peeked out from their hiding spot.

From this distance, they appeared the same, one red, the other black.

He peered back up at the monitor: *seven.*

Darrovan moved around the side of the podium, where he first saw Talcen.

Brelo snagged his arm.

"What are you doing?" she mouthed without sound.

He held up a hand.

"Trust me," he replied in the same manner.

I've seen what your kind does to people. I've seen the horror you've witnessed. Your world's strange, more, and yet less than my own.

Darrovan glanced back up: *four*.

Your kind cannot survive. You pose a threat to my world, and you're all inferior.

The miasma built up, towering above the fountain, poising to strike.

Your world must be eradicated.

The monitor flashed: *two*.

The miasma struck. Stone and water spewed.

Darrovan stood.

He swiped Talcen's badge on the podium, and pressed the button labeled: *security*.

The elevator doors parted with a ding.

Guns dropped from the ceiling.

Darrovan stood.

"Hold out your badge, Brelo!"

The guns swiveled in his direction. He held up his badge and pointed at the miasma.

There you are, Darrovan.

A cackle of glee rose through him. The guns swiveled down the hall. The miasma rolled forward, energy crackling within. Darrovan darted for the elevator. Brelo was already within.

The guns twirled, their barrels rolling. The alien kept coming, halfway to them.

Brelo pressed the close button nonstop.

"Close, damn you!"

By the time the guns opened up, the miasma was almost upon them. A torrent of bright light ripped through the lobby. Lasers pierced the miasma.

Zhidur screamed in agony, filling his head.

"Oh, God, this is going to be close."

The doors started to shut. Brelo frantically moved to the only other button in the lift and started mashing.

The hatch slid shut, and Zhidur's rage and pain ripped through him.

The fury swept over him. His knees buckling. A fresh wave of white-hot pain shot through him as he fell to the floor.

"Darrovan," Brelo called, kneeling beside him.

The lift shook, and she tumbled down beside him.

"We're not going to make it," she said, her voice filled with defeat.

Metal from far below groaned.

The gunfire's noise rose in pitch. The elevator kept ascending. Brelo clutched his hand.

You cannot kill me, Darrovan. I've cheated death before. I will always be.

"You never told me what you planned to do if we made it," she said.

He let out a deep breath. "I think I'll start with a drink."

She gave a single laugh. "And after?"

He opened his mouth to answer, and the lift shook. A deafening roar rose up around them, and the agony that accompanied it devoured him.

Epilogue

Darrovan took a drink from the glass of water in front of him.

Before the events of the Dome, he would've been a nervous wreck, but now that he had faced death and escaped, the gathered delegation seemed trivial by comparison.

He set the glass down. The water sloshing back and forth. He reached up to his tie, pulling on it.

The collar was too tight. He should have bought another shirt.

"You may proceed with your opening statement, Professor Wiev."

Darrovan glanced to the left.

Brelo sat at his side. She looked stunning in her attire. A small smile spread across her lips, and it gave him all the courage he needed.

He leaned forward and punched the mic on.

"Thank you, Mr. Chairman."

He glanced at the panel before him. A dozen lined the curving podium, but many more sat behind.

"I know this goes without saying for the masses, but my profession as an alien theorist is considered more laughable than what a comedian would say. Others say I'm dangerous. I've come to accept that. I chose my profession out of passion and out of wistful hopefulness. While I silently prayed to be proven right, I never dreamed I would be, or the ramifications that came with such a discovery."

He glanced at Brelo again; she reached out, took his hand, and squeezed it.

It'd been one hell of an event just to get here, and the horrors of what happened in that secret base didn't stop at the explosion. What followed … he didn't wish that on anyone.

His eyes darted over her face, noting her soft smile, the warmth in her eyes.

The scars that marred her face had healed into faint lines, but she'd carry them forever, just as they'd carry the memories of what happened. And the blemishes that stained his soul would endure as long as he lived.

"I've come before this body to give a detailed recounting of my brief internment at the abandoned military base dubbed 'the Dome.' It's a tale that'll be smeared in all the papers, retold in tabloids, and laughed about in hushed circles. Yet, I feel that it's incumbent upon me to reveal this deadly threat.

"My wife, Dr. Brelo Wiev, and I, only escaped with our lives. For that, I'm eternally grateful. But the lives lost in the interim can't be so easily forgotten. For the families who lost loved ones, the truth must be told. I won't be mocked, dismissed, or ridiculed into silence. These families deserve answers, and I'll honor those who perished by telling their tale.

"Honored delegates. The threat is real. I've encountered an alien, just one, and that was enough. It went by the name Zhidur, and it was locked away in the vault of the Dome. It came for answers, for information about us, and decided we were a threat. It came for the eradication of the entire sothor species…"

About the Author

Kyle Belote is a prior active-duty Marine, writer, musician, and painter. He's lived in Texas, Hawaii, and Okinawa, Japan, and has traveled the globe. When not writing, he enjoys sketching, researching companies and investing, and reading and listening to audiobooks. Kyle enjoys a diverse collection of films, books, and shows—just not the abomination called Disney Star Wars.

For more information, please visit: www.outpostdire.com